SCIENCE FICTION STORIES AND MORE   OCTOBER 2022

DARKMATTER

MAGAZINE

First paperback edition October 2022.

Edited by Rob Carroll
Cover art by Sean Keeton
Cover design by Rob Carroll
Layout by Rob Carroll

Interior art by Mateus Roberts © 2022,
Zach Horvath copyright © 2022, Rob Carroll copyright © 2022,
Adobe Stock copyright © 2022
Printed by permission.
Promotional images couresy of Del Rey, IDW Publishing, Simon & Schuster

"Trash" by Rob Carroll copyright © 2022,
"Immaterial Witness" by Graham J. Darling copyright © 2022
"The Vampire on the Tesseract Wall" by Larry Hodges copyright © 2022,
"What We Look For at the Night Market" by Ai Jiang copyright © 2021;
originally published March 2022 in *The Dread Machine*
"The Drive" by Jenny Leidecker copyright © 2022,
"Storm Cellar" by Jen Marshall copyright © 2022,
"Shock" by Casey Masterson copyright © 2022,
"Basically Normal" by Scotty Milder copyright © 2022;
"Cube" by Grace R. Reynolds copyright © 2022,
"What Kind of Skin" by Mary G. Thompson copyright © 2022,
"A Piece Missing" by S. J. Townend copyright © 2022
Printed by permission.

Printed by Ingram Content Group

ISBN 978-1-0879-7973-1 (paperback)

Dark Matter Magazine
P.O. Box 372
Wheaton, IL 60187

darkmattermagazine.com
darkmattermagazine.shop

10 9 8 7 6 5 4 3 2 1

SCIENCE FICTION STORIES AND MORE   OCTOBER 2022

DARKMATTER
MAGAZINE

DARK
MATTER

darkmattermagazine.com
darkmattermagazine.shop

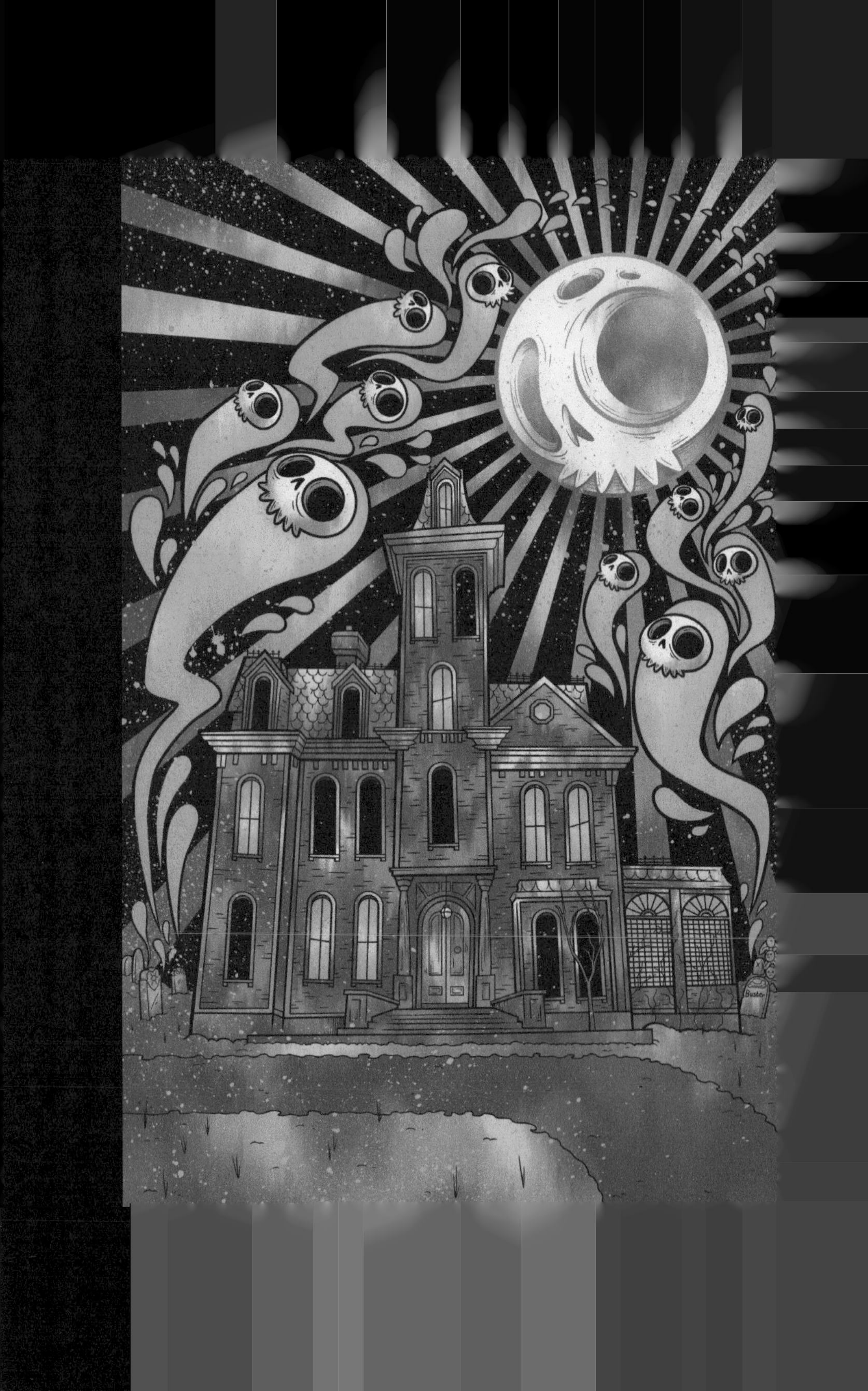
Buster

COVER ART

MYSTERIOUS AND SPOOKY

by Sean Keeton

To experience the "Mysterious and Spooky" image on page 4 in augmented reality (AR): 1) Download the free Artivive app from the Apple App Store or the Google Play store (QR code links below); 2) Open the downloaded app on your device; and 3) With the app open, point your device's camera at the artwork to watch it come to life.

Download via the
Apple App Store

Download via the
Google Play store

Pictured left: *Mysterious and Spooky (Augmented Reality Version)*

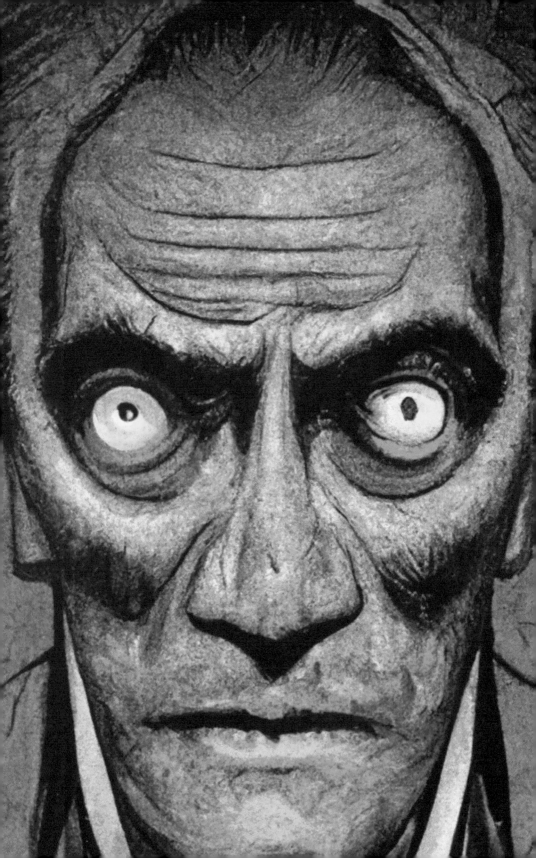

DARK MATTER STAFF

Rob Carroll
Editor-in-Chief

Anna Madden
Acquisitions Editor

Marie Croke
Acquisitions Editor

Marissa van Uden
Acquisitions Editor

Phil McLaughlin
Director of Media

Eric Carroll
Media Relations

Alli Nesbit
Sound Designer

Jena Brown
Features Writer

Olly Jeavons
Illustrator

Janelle Janson
Features Writer

CONTENTS

REPRINT FICTION

AUTHOR INTERVIEWS

ART FEATURES

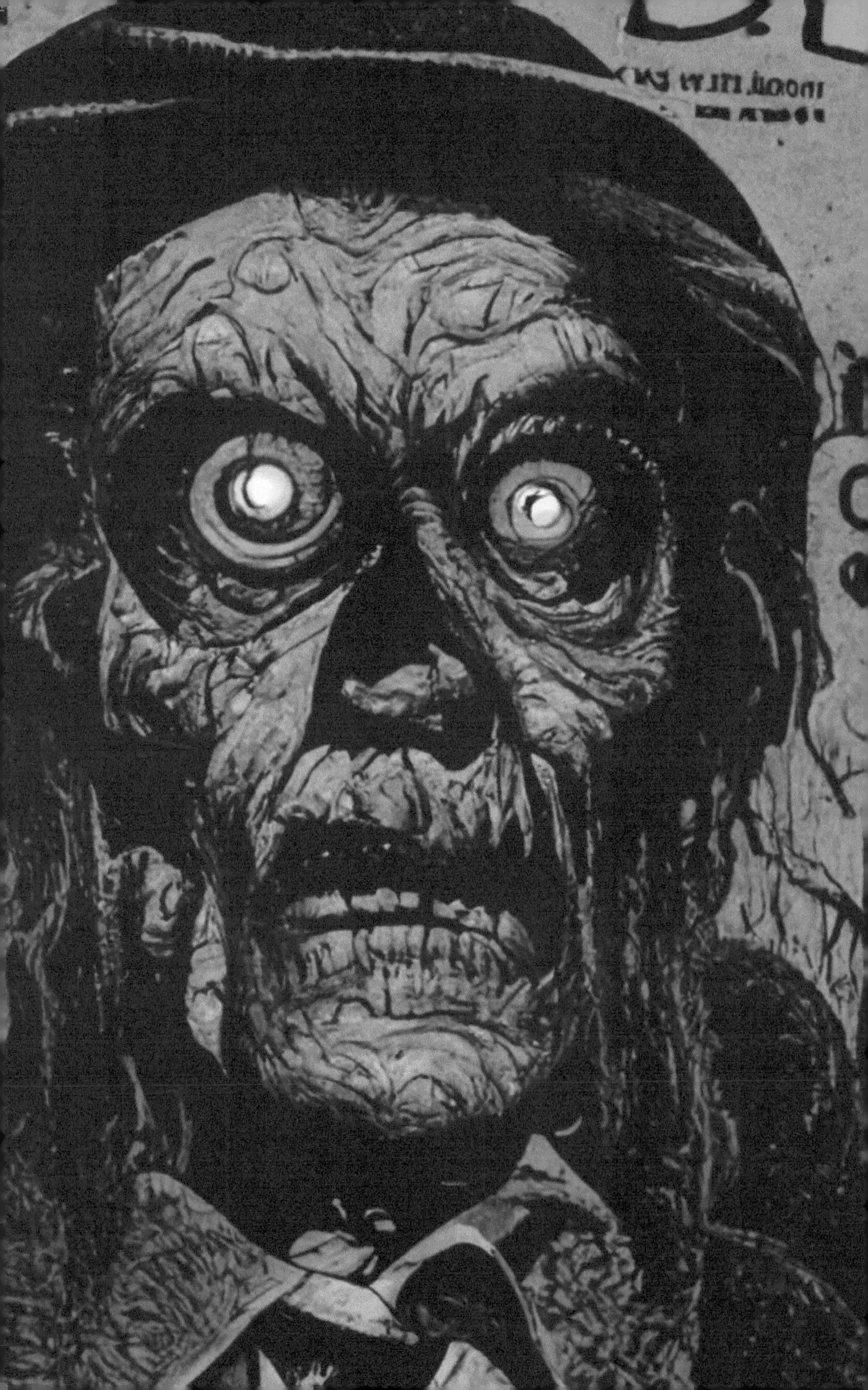

TRASH

by Rob Carroll

G reat American novelist™ Ernest Hemingway once said, "I write one page of masterpiece to ninety-one pages of shit. I try to put the shit in the wastebasket."

When I first stumbled upon this quote some time ago, my first reaction was to chuckle knowingly. My second reaction was to ask myself this question: Is there any more universal feeling among writers than the feeling of total and undefeatable inadequacy? Don't get me wrong; there is a ton of truth to what Hemingway says. Most of our thoughts aren't worth the electricity it takes to make them (just imagine how quickly the world's energy crisis would be solved if we discovered how to turn internet shitposting into a renewable source of energy), but who's to say what's trash? Great American pop artist™ Andy Warhol said, "Art is anything you can get away with." So, by his standard, nothing is trash and everything is art, even the worst paragraph ever written (which would definitely have a Dadaist appeal, if you think about it).

Most writers agree that in order to be good at your craft you have to be even better at knowing what's bad, and I concur. Even in the context of subjectivity, some things just aren't up to a certain standard, and that's both true and artistically healthy to admit. If you can't admit that, you'll quite simply cease to improve. But don't worry, I'm not here to decide what's trash. I'm here to champion it.

Yeah, Hemingway is right. Most stuff we create is garbage (mostly because it has to follow the impossible-to-follow act known as ALL OF CREATION), but you know what, sometimes garbage is good. And sometimes, it's even the most authentic art we create, the stuff that most effortlessly emulates our natural state of being—flawed and confused, frustrated, annoyed, just trying to make it one day at a time by figuring everything out on the fly. You know, human.

This is the magic of pulp fiction, of cult classics, of the miraculous game-winning base hit that is looped off the end of the bat and falls gently in between infielder and outfielder for a heroic walk-off single by the bench player batting .225 on the season. There is no pretense in these works, no assumption made by the person wielding the pen, the movie camera, or the baseball bat that what they're making is the pinnacle of artistic or athletic achievement. There is simply action. And then later, reaction. And whatever happens between the former and latter points in time is left bravely for fate to decide.

Genre fiction—whether it be science fiction, fantasy, crime, horror, or the like—has been accused on occasion of being garbage fiction, pulpy trash, the reading equivalent of junk food. Those that write it write for money, and those that read it just don't know any better. There have been numerous attempts to "elevate" or "legitimize" genre fiction in response, but the one thing all these movements have in common is that they seem to miss the point.

Genre fiction is emotion distilled—science fiction is wonder, fantasy is awe, horror is fear, etc.—and you can't elevate something that already exists in its purest form. You can mine the elements and mix them to create an alloy, but the ore that is Genre will remain singularly unchanged.

A story about a giant man-eating spider the size of a Ford F-150 might not win the National Book Award, but it will speak directly to what's in the creator's heart and mind in a way that is undeniably authentic (either the writer is really afraid of spiders, they really love the idea of spider revenge, or they really want to cash in on the new giant spider craze sweeping Hollywood). Could the story be executed terribly and need a rewrite? Sure. Could it be a soulless corporate cash grab? Sure. But is it trash? I think that's for the author and their fellow lovers of spider-revenge fiction to decide.

In this, the second annual Halloween Special Issue of *Dark Matter*, ten stories look genre fiction in the eye and smile with anticipatory glee. Every tale within these pages adds its own bit of artistic flair, but at the root of all these works is an undeniable love for telling stories that make us wince, gasp, jump, laugh, cringe, groan, chuckle, smirk, sigh, shiver, and even shake our heads in disbelief. They weave fearless narratives that entertain as much as they impress.

"What Kind of Skin" by Mary G. Thompson explores the cynical human urge to rationalize one's harmful actions in the name of self-preservation, and does so with a very creepy story about aliens. "Cube" by Grace R. Reynolds makes literal the destructive ways we use and exploit each other in our utilitarian systems, as told by an insane university professor and his classroom of burgeoning sociopaths. "The Drive" by Jenny Leidecker toys with the old horror trope of the mysterious hitchhiker at night via clever use of perspective and a wickedly funny final act. "Basically Normal" by Scotty Milder is another darkly humorous tale that throws a serial killer into a comedy-of-errors plot while also posing interesting questions about the erroneous ways we define ourselves, sometimes to the detriment of others. "Storm Cellar" by Jen Marshall is a gut-punch of a tale about fathers, sons, and the struggle between modern and traditional masculinity, but with a mysterious monster and a terrorized small town at the heart of it all. "Shock" by Casey Masterson is a true throwback to the *Creepshow*, *Tales From the Crypt* era of horror, and Masterson's deft use of shock (no pun intended) and humor is sure to have the reader groaning at the cringe-worthy portrait of human folly that she paints. "The Vampire on the Tesseract Wall" by Larry Hodges is a fourth dimension mind-trip that uses aliens and vampires to tackle questions about voyeurism, power structures, and the nature of reality itself. "Immaterial Witness" by Graham J. Darling is a ghost story about bureaucracy and how even death is powerless to stop its overreach. "A Piece Missing" by S. J. Townend is a psychological horror story about grief, memory, and regret that unfolds like an elegant tapestry, one jaw-dropping reveal at a time. And finally, this issue's reprint story, "What We Look For at the Night Market" by Ai Jiang is like a Hideo Miyazaki film about all the borderlands in our lives and how they act not as barriers, but as retreats from the sadness that haunts the waking world.

Sincerely,

Rob Carroll
Editor-in-Chief

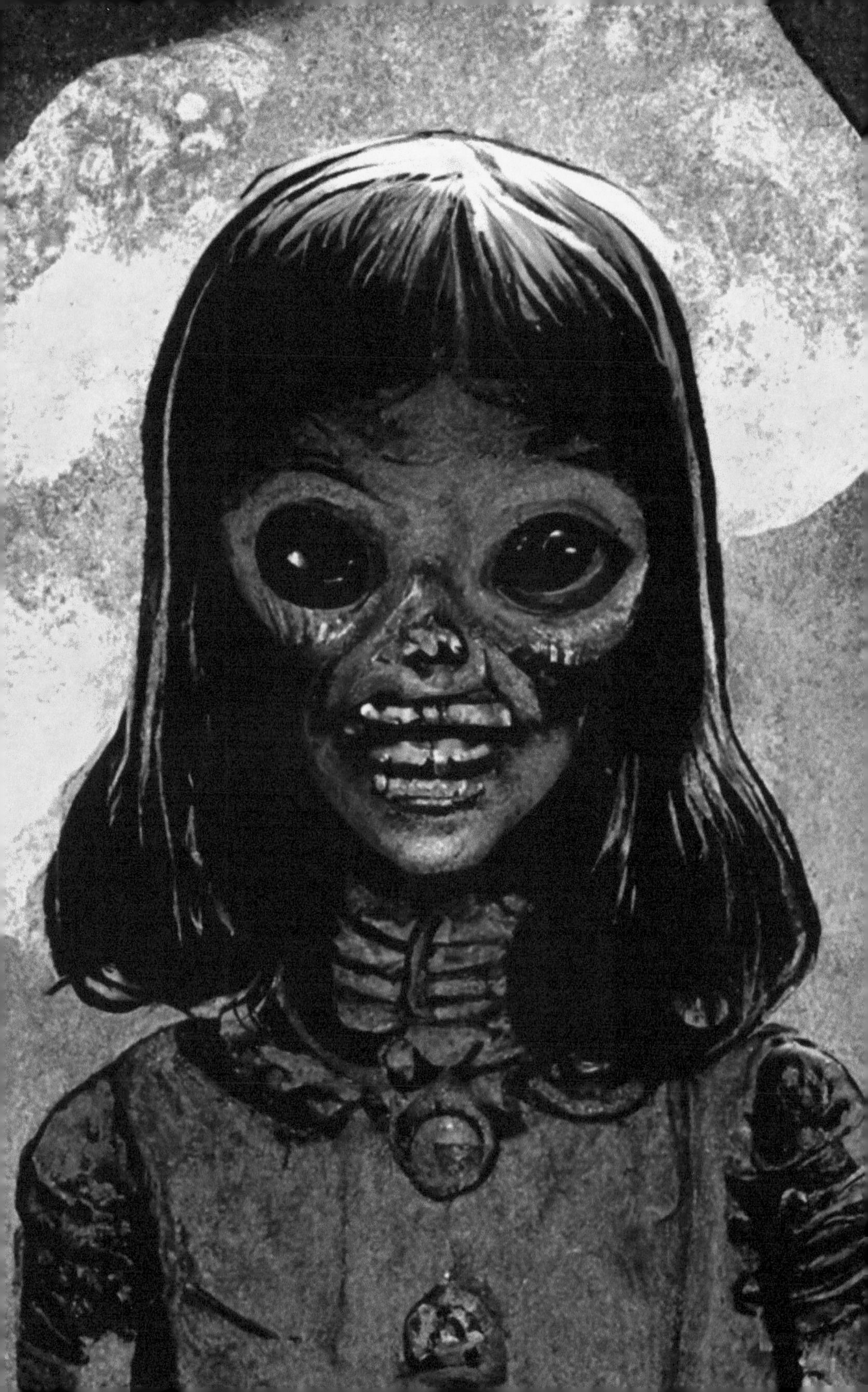

WHAT KIND OF SKIN

by Mary G. Thompson

John comes home from work at 9:00 p.m. I've just gotten Alexandra to bed. She's had trouble sleeping recently, with her sensitive skin and the cold weather.

John is moving slowly. He gets tired at night, especially after eating all that meat they give him at the office. He needs his greens as much as I do. I used to fix them for him, but he wouldn't eat. He would say he ate already, and it isn't as if I want him to eat here in front of me. Of course I don't want that. But I do want him to be healthy.

He shakes his coat off onto the table in the foyer, and I pick it up and hang it. I have to brush the inside, which worries me. There's skin coming off his neck in noticeable amounts lately. But I don't mention it. He knows already, of course. It's his body.

"How was your day?" I ask. I'm standing; he's sitting in the big chair, the recliner. It's black leather, and skin from his head and neck is shedding like snow. Pretty, really, under the low light. It could be.

His green eyes stare back at me. He blinks. "It was another good day."

"Not too cold," I say. I sit down on the couch across from him. It's hard to sit back, hard to relax. He stares at me with those eyes. They're stunning eyes, really. I thought in the beginning, I could look at those eyes. Wouldn't it be nice if my children had eyes like that? I have boring brown eyes. Nobody wants eyes like mine.

"It is often too cold for me," he says.

We sit quietly. I want to offer him a drink, something to break the silence. But he doesn't need that. Behind those green eyes, under the sharply defined cheekbones and the thick dark hair, he's thinking. He's using a mind I have no window into.

Behind John, the outline of the city rises. The lights are magnificent from this height. Spectacular. I can see the whole thing. I never dreamed, when I was Alexandra's age, that I would ever have a view like this. This couch I'm sitting on cost $13,000. Just for the one piece. How could I ever have imagined?

"How is Alex-andra," he asks. There's a break in his pronunciation of her name. He has some difficulty with it. Long words, sometimes, are hard for their stiff tongues. And it doesn't sound like a question. They don't really understand how we do questions.

"She's finally sleeping."

"It is time to make an attempt."

"Yes." I catch my body stiffening, and before the tension can take hold, I leap to my feet. I've been through this many times, and it's all right. I reach out for John's hand, looking out the window from the corner of my eye, on the beautiful view. Down there, beneath the lights, is where I lived once. With my first husband and my first daughter, I existed. It was a much colder night than this one when John came walking through the courtyard. Him, in his long wool coat with his green eyes. Me, in my ripped old puffer on a bench. All it took was an examination in the cleanest doctor's office I'd ever seen. She pronounced me healthy.

John kisses me on the cheek. "I love you, Liv." His voice is even, and what he thinks he means when he says that is no one's guess.

"I love you too," I say. I smile, although he doesn't. I kiss him gently on the cheek, and my lips come away with the tiniest of flakes on them. Which is all right. Because they're beautiful, really. Almost like snow.

John doesn't mind the darkness.

Once, when I was married to a man I met in school, who had warm flesh and a soft and supple tongue, I liked to keep the lights on. I reveled in the experiences of the senses, my eyes taking in the curve of his flesh, the light of his brown eyes, the fold of the bedspread as the frame rattled.

Now I run my hands down John's back, although I'm not sure if he feels it. He has never said not to or asked for it to be a different way. I want him on top, because that way I won't see as much. This action mars his skin, breaks it, rubs it off. It exposes him for who he is. But underneath him, I close my eyes. I let my hands dig into him. I press myself up. I imagine I am somewhere, with someone. And he is strong. He is strong enough to break me. I could break myself against him, and maybe I will. I am warm, and he is cold. He presses down against me and makes almost no noise. I too make no noise, although I sweat into the sheets. I'm weak from exertion.

I cling to him. I press my palms against the roughness of his back's surface, against the truth of who he is, revealed. My eyes have adjusted to the low light, and over his shoulder, I see the gray circular scales, repeating down the small of his back over his buttocks, which are still partly covered by human skin.

When I scattered my husband's ashes over my daughter's grave, I thought I would never feel this again. I thought I would never touch another man.

A noise comes from his mouth that doesn't sound like language to me. I've tried to learn it. I've studied audio. But the clicks and hisses bounce around in my ears. He rolls off me, serpentine and scaly, eyes still the beautiful perfect green, head full of human hair intact. He hisses at me.

"Of course," I say. Because I don't understand the words, and yet I do. I, naked and sweaty, still with my skin, roll off the bed. In his presence, I almost curve when I walk. I slink to the closet and retrieve the cream. It's a large bin. It's so large it takes up the entire half of the closet. Like a barrel you'd put soup in for a block full of hungry humans. I scoop up as much of it as I can carry in my hands and climb on the bed. I cross my legs, revel in the skin of one leg touching the genuine skin of the other, press my hand to his back. Slowly, I rub the cream in.

His back, his stomach, his arms, his legs. It takes time to cover his body; it takes time to wash him all away. Finally, I touch his face. I run my thumbs along his cheekbones. I rub my fingers into his scalp. I close my eyes.

When I open them, there is the man staring back, the man who rescued me when I was starving and cold. He has smooth ivory skin and long lush lashes. Perfect teeth and a tongue that looks human unless you look closely. On his breath is the faint remnant of raw flesh.

He hisses at me, and I press my face into his shoulder.

"Do you believe it was successful," he asks.

"I hope so," I say.

"I am assigned to have a second offspring by thirteen moons."

"Yes."

"Our offspring will be many."

"They won't have to live this way," I say. "No more creams. No more business suits."

"I will always protect you, Liv." He presses a hand against my neck as if he's going to caress my head. I don't know where he learned that. It's like when he says *I love you*. He's trying to be what he thinks I need.

"I know."

John curls up under the blankets. He has a special one, electric, that he wraps around his lower body. It radiates heat, which is sometimes overwhelming. I lie with just a sheet over me, and as his breathing settles into sleep, I wait. It's rare for sleep to come to me before the clock ticks past midnight. This has always been true. Before my husband and I both lost our jobs, before the power went out, before … I don't even think her name, in the darkness, in the privacy of my mind.

Alexandra lets out a high-pitched hiss. I hear it through two sets of walls. It's as if the noises she makes when she's upset are specially tuned to reach my ears; not John's, mine. He doesn't wake.

Her room is hot and humid, almost swampy. They need it that way when they're young, John says. As they get older, they become better able to adapt to a place with varying seasons, like this part of Earth. Children like Alexandra are supposed to be able to adapt better: earlier, more completely.

"Mom?"

"I'm here. What's going on?" I sit on the side of her bed. She's sitting too. Her head is bathed in the city lights. She has brown hair like mine and his green eyes. Her skin is a combination: not scales, not smooth, not pale and pinkish, not gray. She needs the cream to fit into the world, for now. Someday, she won't have to use it. When there are fewer human babies, she'll be able to come out of the shadows. And someday there will be no humans. There will be none of them either. There will be only the children.

"My back itches."

There's a smaller container of the cream under her bed. She lifts her shirt, and I carefully rub it into her back. For these children, itching is like growing pains are for us. It happens; it's harmless; it will pass.

She hisses a sound that I know means contentment.

I shiver. It's too hot for me in here, and yet every time I touch her skin, I feel cold. Her face is turned up toward the window. I pray she can't see my reflection. I pray she never learns to read the minute contours of my face. Because I love her. She's my daughter as much as his.

I slide into the bed next to her and wrap my arm around her shoulders. "Feel better?"

"Yeah. I just wish it would stop itching all the time."

"It will." We look out the window together. In the distance, a helicopter flies over the tall buildings. Most likely, it's manned by them. It will be a long time still before the whole world knows they're here, before Alexandra and hopefully, my future children, are the survivors. Down there in the darkest corners of the city, where I once lived, more and more people die every day. But not me. As long as I continue producing children for them, I'll be safe. I'll be able to live here with electricity, food, clean water, furnishings. I'll have medical care. And so will my children.

"Mom?"

"Yeah?"

"How come you never have to use the cream?"

"Well, I have a different kind of skin."

"What kind?"

Human, I think. But I'm not sure I get to say that. The word no longer applies to me. "The kind that doesn't feel as much," I say instead.

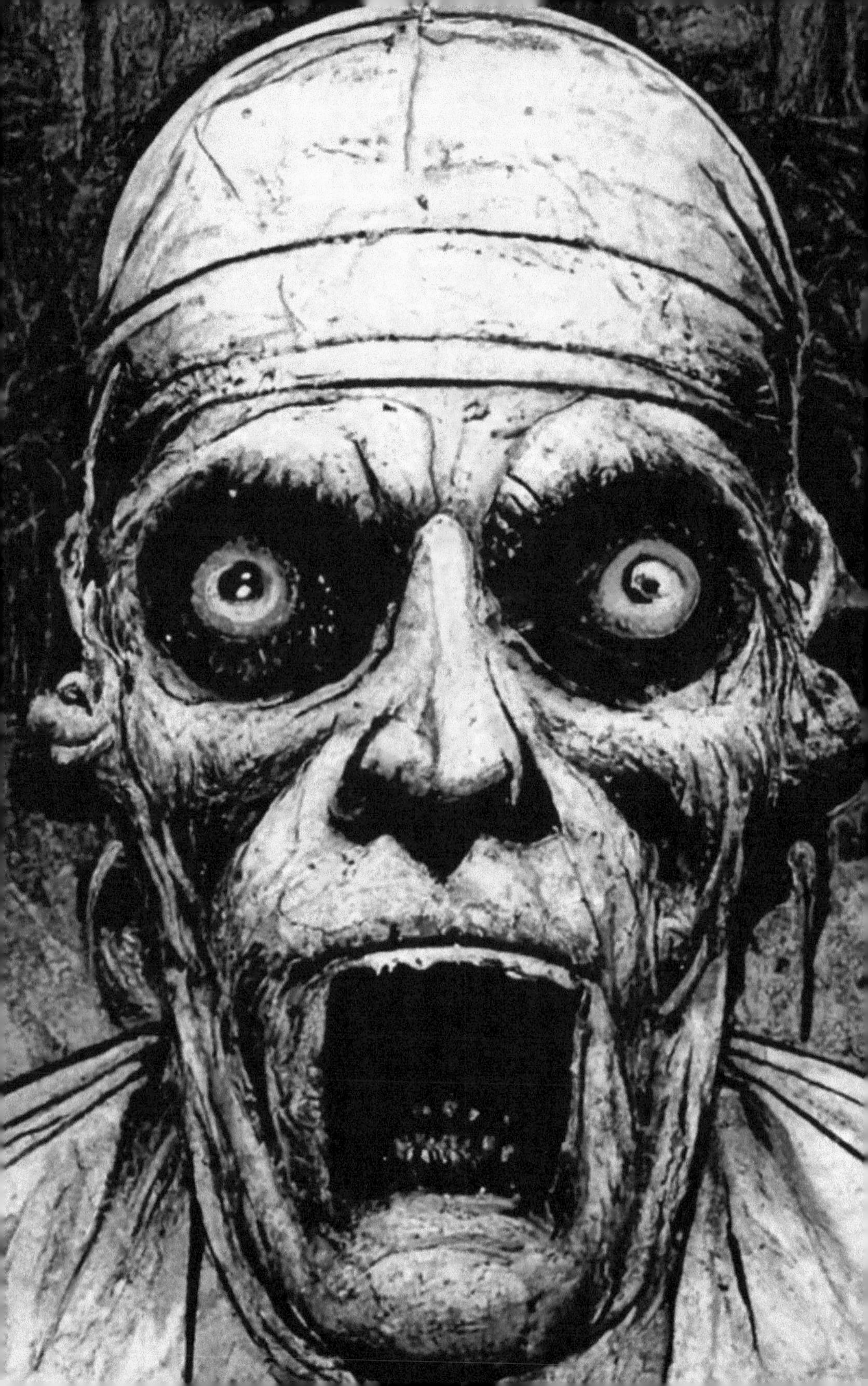

CUBE

by Grace R. Reynolds

In the center of an art studio, painted in the purest shade of white, is a man. The man is naked. He is shaved of all the existing hairs on his body and strapped to a tilt table inclined at a sixty-degree angle. His eyes are kept open with the assistance of metallic ophthalmic speculums, and there is an IV attached to his wrist. Next to the man is a smaller table complete with various surgical tools. At the end of a scalpel are the fiddling fingers of a Dr. Ogden. He waits patiently for his students to finish their rendition of their subject this week.

"Surrender your brush, everyone. Let us examine your interpretation of the subject before us."

Outside of this classroom, the man can exist as whoever he wants to be. However, the man belongs to the Collective and has been stripped of any previous sense of agency. Within these walls, the Collective has studied and dictated his human experience over the last three weeks.

The students sit in a semicircle around the life form, their aprons smeared in strokes of acrylic paint that range in various colors. No color stands out as that of the shades, most notably red. A most vicious and lascivious shade of red. The students are not to exchange academic discourse over color; however, their primary focus is the cubes of flesh on the plates next to their easels.

"Tell me, class, how have the cubes on your plates changed over the last three weeks? What is it that you see beyond the three-dimensional shape? Your rendition this week should reflect what it is you would tell us about our dear creature here."

Dr. Ogden gestures to the subject reverently and approaches the tilt table. The instructor stretches out his hand to touch the figure and, with gangly fingers, lazily traces the scared edges of the series of wounds over the left arm of its body. When Dr. Ogden reaches the subject's hand, he briefly inspects the IV to ensure it is still correctly in place before he continues. A student warily raises their hand.

"Ah, yes, a volunteer. Do share with us your observations."

The student turns their easel around to face the rest of the Collective. A loosely painted structure on their canvas vaguely resembles the bloated shape next to them. The image bubbles with layers of pink, yellow, and red. It could be mistaken for a bit of candy if one does not look too closely at the thing.

"Interesting color palette. Last week the cubes looked more green in color, wouldn't you agree?"

"Well, that's what color it was last week, sir. This week it's red."

"Can you indulge us further? What have you noticed about the cubes' transformations?"

The student pauses for a moment before selecting their words. "I suppose the color change is a result of the decomposition of the human body."

Dr. Ogden has become visibly agitated by the student's lazy response to his query. He takes a deep breath, firmly clasps his hands, and purses his lips.

"Of course, it is a result of decomposition. However, are we not studying more than the likeness of skin and muscle? Can you, or rather, can anyone share with the Collective what it is that we are really exploring and observing in the cube?"

The Collective sits in silence. Perhaps they are afraid to say the wrong thing, or worse, they are scared to utter the correct answer. How can they bring themselves to validate that which Dr. Ogden has sought for them to understand?

Dr. Ogden approaches the wary student's easel to study the canvas once more. He furrows his brow and places his hand on their shoulder. The student's body tenses under his touch, but Dr. Ogden does not retract. Instead, he speaks once more.

"Come. Instead of me trying to spoon-feed you the answer to our study, let me show you."

The organism on the tilt table follows the two of them with his eyes. As they approach the living subject, Dr. Ogden centers the student squarely in front of the being before holding his hand up, indicating to the student to stop moving. Dr. Ogden stands at their side and gestures for the student to meet the flesh donor's gaze.

"Look into this man's eyes. Over the past three weeks, he has been in your presence, yet it is clear that you do not see what it is he has yielded to you. We will have to start over with your teaching until you fully grasp that which he has acquiesced in the name of art."

Dr. Ogden picks up a scalpel from the small table next to them and hands it to the student. The student looks at him in horror, knowing what Dr. Ogden would instruct them to do, and declines with their silence. Dr. Ogden offers the scalpel again, but the student objects once more and holds up their hand. Dr. Ogden's face scrunches, and he says, with intense scorn, "How dare you! How dare you deny that which the man has given you!" Before the student can muster up the courage to verbally object this time, Dr. Ogden has dug the scalpel's blade into the subject's arm.

The donor's eyes widen in surprise. Their teeth gnash, and their eyes flare in agony as they struggle against the ophthalmic speculums. They look at the student who defied Dr. Ogden's direction to blame their peer. The student whirls around the classroom and looks upon the Collective.

"This is sick! I didn't sign up for this!"

"Oh, but you did. Do you mean to tell me that you have sat idly by these last few weeks, unaware of our activities here? Does culpability only apply to the individual with the scalpel in hand?" Dr. Ogden completes his incision and sets down the scalpel. He then picks up a pair of tissue forceps and motions to the Collective to lift their paintbrushes. The Collective obeys as one and begins to mix colors on their palettes in shades of that most vicious red.

Dr. Ogden removes the fresh cube of muscle with precision and holds it in the air. A different student leaves their post to offer their plate to him to lay the cube on it. He bows his head in thanks and smoothes his hair back as if what has just occurred does not faze him in the slightest. He ignores the defiant student, who is now kneeling over in a ball, silently sobbing on the floor.

"I will ask again, can anyone tell me why it is that we are studying the shape of the cube in this context? *Anyone?*" He waits again while his patience begins to wane. Another student raises her hand in hesitation.

"Go on, yes?"

The young student clears her throat and stands up to project her voice better for the room.

"Well, sir, in art fundamentals, we learned that the cube teaches us how to master the characteristics of a subject, such as the edges, face, and angles."

"Yes, but please, tell me what it symbolizes beyond its mathematics. Dig deeper!"

Sweat prickles Dr. Ogden's brow as he anxiously awaits the student's answer. He looks at the clock. Only fifteen minutes remaining in the day.

"The shape of the cube is a stable and permanent structure. In the form of flesh, though, it is no longer permanent. Its stability fluctuates through the process of decomposition—" the student pauses. A smile creeps across her face as she makes the connection between thoughts. "—As does life."

"Excellent!" Dr. Ogden pumps his fist in the air. At last, finally, a student that can follow his train of thought!

"Dear Collective, take a mental note here. What is existence, if not instinct to build a world around us to survive? Look, look at the man! The tears rolling down his face are not merely just an indicator of his pain. They are a marker of the body's signal to survive, and what has his body done these past few weeks? It has begun the healing process in the pits where I have dug my blade. Is there not beauty in that?"

The student whom he had engaged with becomes evangelized. Tears of joy stream down her face with this new sense of knowledge. The remainder of the Collective sitting in their semicircle stands and begins to applaud the revelation bestowed upon them. The room is filled with echoes of clapping that reverberate against the walls. At this moment, the student balled up on the floor before their subject screams.

"What is wrong with you? All of you? Is this some kind of cult? SADISTS!"

The student scrambles to their feet. They lunge toward the being on the table in an attempt to rip the IV out from their wrist. Before they can grab it, Dr. Ogden strikes them down by piercing the muscle between their shoulder and collarbone with the scalpel.

The student's skin pales and becomes clammy as they double over on the floor. Their heart pumps furiously in their chest. An overwhelming sense of nausea takes over, and they vomit on the floor in front of the Collective.

Dr. Ogden hoists the student onto their knees. He holds their head to look up at the creature on the tilt table. The being's eyes are bloodshot, silently lamenting for the student to comply.

"This man has allowed you to exercise that which the greatest men of history have all sought, and you deny it! Why do you deny what is freely being given to you? I urge you to take what is yours! You *will* take what is yours!"

"And what the hell is that supposed to be?" the student seethes, their face wrought with tears and saliva.

Dr. Ogden looks upon them with disgust as if he is the one bearing the subject's scabbed-over wounds, or perhaps the one freshly bleeding, rather than the student.

"Even after your peer here gave you bread crumbs, you dare tell us that you still do not understand the true nature of our exploration here? Do you not know what this man has presented unto you as your right, divine, and in line with the natural order?"

"Stop talking in riddles!"

"Power; the assertion of your will over those who do not want it."

Another student innocently chimes in, "But Dr. Ogden, what does that have to do with power? Is this more than a representation of mortality?"

Dr. Ogden acknowledges the student's request. "There is a quote, often attributed to a famous psychoanalyst, that says 'most people do not really want freedom, because freedom involves responsibility, and most people are frightened of responsibility.' Take this man, for example. He came here of his own free will to participate in a study advertised in the university newspaper in exchange for 'the basic necessities of living.' That was all the advertisement said. We know nothing else about the man other than this. Now tell me. Will you argue with that logic? Are you going to tell me that this man truly values the responsibility of living if he so blindly accepted this call to art?"

In their fit of grief, pain, and confusion, the student has become un-aware of the Collective closing in on them. They are forced to their feet; the scalpel is placed into their hands. Dr. Ogden's fingers wrap around theirs, and together, they both draw the tip of the blade ever closer to the man's torso.

"You will take what is yours! Take it! Take it!"

"NO! NO, NO, NO, NO, NO!"

The Collective chants behind them, "TAKE IT. TAKE IT. TAKE IT. TAKE IT."

The student scuttles, their eyes tremble, and they strain against the being before them. The scalpel inches away, the student lingers and catches glimpses between the man's glazed eyes and the blade. The student's palms sweat, their pulse palpitating against the instrument's handle. The scalpel digs deep into the figure's right arm, unmarred by previous incisions. Voices of the Collective's chant ring and bellow within their fevered ears. The student closes their eyes, grits their teeth, and shrieks as they feel the incision trace the distinct shape of a square, followed by a deeper cut to create a cube.

"Dear Collective! This man has given up his agency for our sake! Has he learned the value of the responsibility of life?"

"Yes!" chimes the Collective.

"Then let this be the last of it, and we shall let him go on his way, free to exist once more in the world as he sees fit."

A man sits in a community center, passing the time alone. He is drinking a cup of coffee while checking his bank account on his phone. He smiles assuringly, knowing that he is secure financially, and returns the phone to the pocket from whence it came. From the corner of his eye, he notices a woman staring. She is looking at the scars on his arm.

He pulls down the cuff of his sleeve to cover the marks and walks over to her. She is shy at first, but soon enough, they are talking. Their chat results in exchanging phone numbers, and the man is on his way. His heart radiates with tenderness and delight from the encounter. The man studies the new number and reminisces about the conversation and the woman's beauty. While in this state of mind, his eyes anchor upon his phone. The light from it emits and snaps him into reality. He glares at his phone but quickly observes the time. The man holds his breath, narrows his gaze, and bites his lip. His lips sink into his mouth; he locks his phone and realizes he will be late for class if he does not hurry.

The man's footsteps reverberate throughout the halls. He halts outside the door of the room and approaches a locker. He turns his combination to open the door and finds a pure white jumpsuit inside. The man leaves his belongings and dresses in the jumpsuit before shutting the locker door.

The man turns the handle and is met by the image of a semicircle of students sitting around art easels. He nods to Dr. Ogden to take his place before the lecture begins. In front of him are a blank canvas and a plate of flesh in the shape of a cube.

"Good morning, Collective."

"Good morning, Dr. Ogden."

In the middle, there is a figure lying on a tilt table. Naked, shaved of all the hairs on their body. Outside the classroom, the figure might be recognized as the student reticent to participate in the Collective the week prior. This week, however, they are no one and only belong to the Collective. Dr. Ogden picks up his scalpel and draws the tip of his blade closer to the figure's skin while the previous week's subject sits before the new sacrifice.

The man, who only recently reclaimed his humanity, picks up his brush and begins to paint.

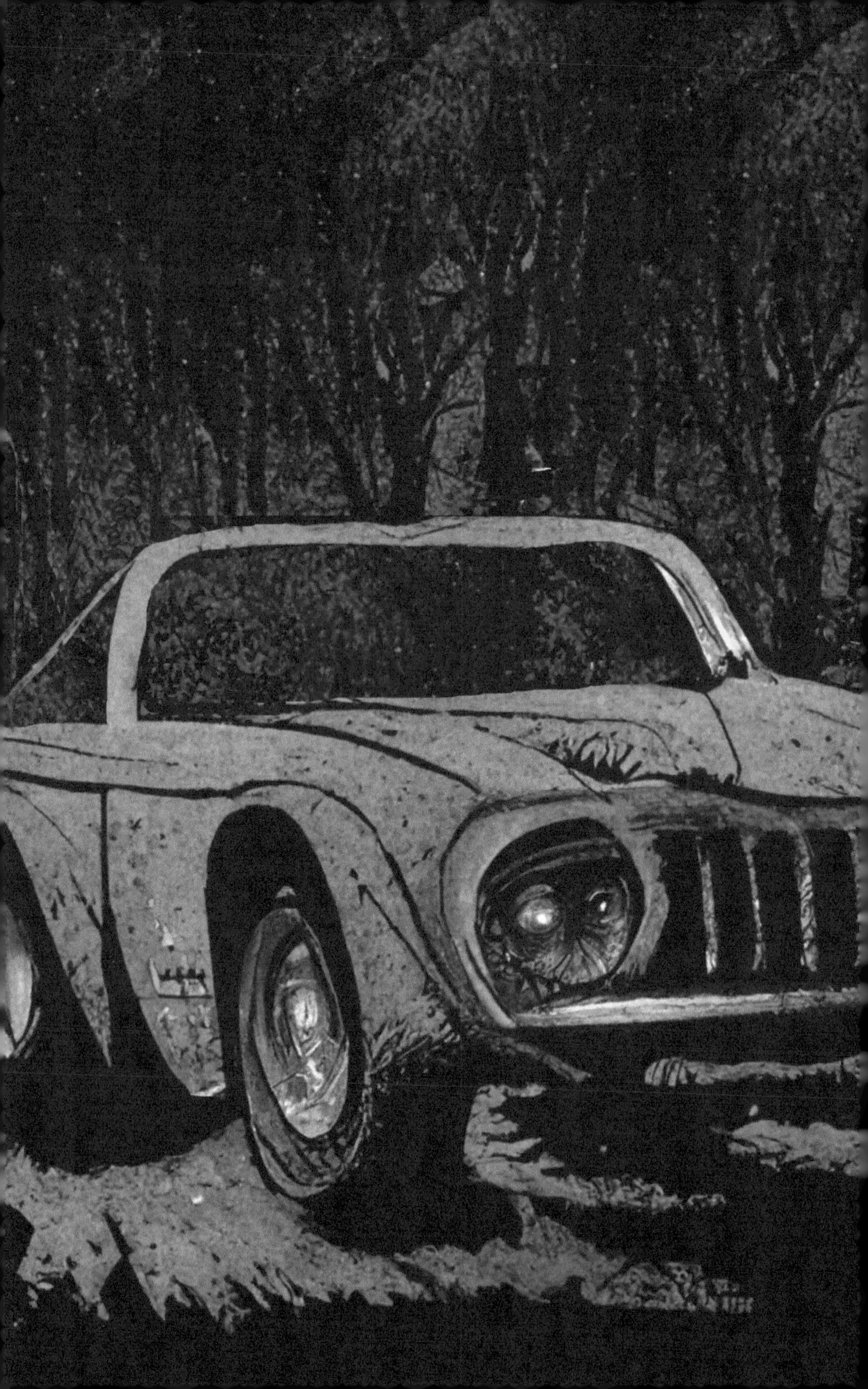

THE DRIVE

by Jenny Leidecker

I'm not sure what I was thinking as I was driving down the highway. My thoughts had been wandering all over the place. You know those moments when you're completely lost in some other world inside your head and how when you finally come to, you've driven miles with no memory of how you ended up where you are? That's the place I had been lost in for God only knows how long. I'm amazed that I haven't gone careening off a cliff, or driven into a ditch, or simply rammed into the back of someone else's car. So far, so good, though. Not my typical trip into the void, that's for sure, and not one I should visit often either. I just think the isolation of driving alone at night along this relatively empty highway has led my imagination off into some unusually twisted scenarios. Only a vague sense of survival holds them all together. Survival is the goal for everyone, isn't it? I'm pretty sure life is just a game of who can live longer, and even though there are a lot of people losing in today's day and age, I'd still prefer to keep playing for a while longer.

Perhaps I just know it's all going to be alright, or maybe I'm just in the mood to tempt fate a little for once instead of feeling controlled by her plan, but in what can only be described as a lapse of judgment, I find myself pulling over and picking up this strange man who has been walking there on the side of the highway. There's nothing for miles, and a storm is working its way in this direction. "Help your fellow man" is still one of those things we're supposed to do, right? And we all take a leap of faith every now and again, don't we? I've never done anything like this before. I know my mother is somewhere clutching her pearls at the mere idea of me noticing some man hitchhiking on the side of the road, much less picking him up. You learn early on as a little girl that it's dangerous being a woman. Not out there in the wild with bears or mountain lions. Those are easy to avoid. No, I'm talking about right here in the everyday world with all these biped creatures born with a Y chromosome. In this world, women learn to traverse the streets always alert to the potential predator around the next corner, and I'm positive that one of the rules etched in those stone tablets is, "Thou shall not pick up hitchhikers." Well, rules be damned. I'm willing to give this one the benefit of the doubt. Surely, he's not out to kill some random woman driving by. I mean, how do you even prepare for that possibility? It can't be easy. Was he just walking there, fingers crossed that some idiot like me would pick him up? *Probably.*

Pulling over onto the shoulder, I run through every scenario in a split second and consider driving off before he can reach the door, but it's too late, and I smile up at the man peering in at me. I can only assume he's consulting his own survival handbook, which doesn't take long, since to him, I'm obviously not a threat. I'm just some woman who's dumb enough to pull over and let him in my car. I should know better. I do know better. He smiles and thanks me as he slides into the seat, shoving his backpack between his knees and holding his hands up to the heating vents to warm his fingers for a bit. Smiling again, he asks where I'm headed, and I let him know I've got at least another hundred miles to cover tonight before I make it to my destination. He's just grateful that he's going to end up that much closer to his own destination before the sun comes up.

I can't imagine traveling like that. Always at someone's mercy, always taking the risk of climbing into a stranger's car. I can tell he does this often by how quickly he relaxes sitting next to me. What does he have to worry about? I'm the one taking the risk this time. I guess he's trying to make me feel more comfortable by sitting back and attempting to hold a casual conversation. However, all I can think about is how I instantly landed in enemy territory the second he opened the passenger door and began to assess every possibility of the situation I had just volunteered for like an idiot.

I keep scanning him out of the corner of my eye. At one point, I see something flickering in the light, exposing what could only be metal at his waist. Is it a knife? Holy crap. What if it *is* a knife? *Of course, it is.* I can't expect someone out on the road at night, willing to jump in the car with a total stranger, not to be armed in some manner. All those thoughts from before start banging around inside my head, and every possibility plays like a movie. How quickly could I react if he grabs for it and sets it up against my throat? Surely, he wouldn't hurt me, at least not while I'm driving. Right? That'd be a stupid decision. Those are the actions that would end up with both of us dead, and quickly too. No, as long as I'm driving, he wouldn't threaten me like that, or at least I don't think he would.

I imagine a hundred different scenarios of what could happen if he pulls that knife from his waistband. I imagine him pulling the knife only to then use it to dig out the dirt from beneath his fingernails (looking at his hands, that wouldn't be such a bad idea). I imagine him using the knife to cut off that loose string from the cuff of his hoodie. But what if he pulls the knife, points it at my neck, forces me to pull over, and tells me all the horrible things he will do to me once I do. Would he force me from the car and leave me there on the side of the road? That's a highly unlikely scenario. Surely, he'd kill me first. But how? Slit my throat from ear to ear? That seems like a messy option. He'd have do that outside the car. I can't see how sitting in a puddle of my blood here on the driver's seat would be a smart plan. He'd want to get out of the car eventually, and it's kind of difficult to hide a bloodstain that big on a pair of jeans. Hell, it's difficult enough to hide those small stains when you find yourself leaking or unprepared. And, well, I'd suspect this would be a much bigger issue than any of those I've experienced. No, he'd have to pull me out of the car first so he wouldn't make a real mess in here. Right?

How, though? I mean, it's not like he can get out and come around the car to make me. I know I'd be scared as hell, but I'd like to think that if he got out of the car, I'd drive off before he could get to me. Of course, an intelligent attacker would take my keys first, and if that were the case, I'd be screwed for sure. Thinking of all the items within reach of me, the closest thing to a weapon I might grab is an umbrella, and surely that damn thing has wiggled its way under the seat too far for me to grab easily. Nope, there's nothing, and I'd be screwed. Maybe I could get to his knife first? I know it's there.

What if I just reached over and grabbed it now? I wonder if he'd react as quickly as he'd need to in order to keep from being in danger? I doubt it. I'm just some woman sitting here, chauffeuring him closer to his destination.

He'd never think I'd do something like that. I wonder if he's the kind of man that would think I was reaching for his…well, you know. I push all of those ridiculous and fear-fed thoughts out of my head. I don't have anything to worry about. He's been friendly so far and not threatening in any way. I'm just letting the entire situation get to me, and I really should focus on driving, or I'm going to get us both killed.

I'm not exactly sure what he had been talking about while my mind was off in "what if" land. Something about his family, I think. He's either on his way to see them, or on a mission to escape them. I'd be lying if I said I knew. We've been driving for a while now, and my stop is only another half-hour down the road. This passenger, did he even tell me his name? Surely he did. Probably just another thing he said that I hadn't paid any attention to because my mind keeps walking in and out of possibilities. I think it's something simple like Joe or Jack, and honestly, it doesn't really matter. It isn't like we were going to be friends and hang out when this ride is all over, that much I know for sure.

I regret the decision to pick him up more and more, with every word he speaks. I should have known better than to think I was up for spending so much time with one person in such close proximity. I'm not really what you'd call a people person, and I know it. I guess I didn't expect him to talk the entire time. I thought maybe he'd catch a few winks or at least take a breath and shut up for a few minutes, but not this one. A real Chatty Cathy, he is. I think about kicking him out more than once along the way, but instead, I sit and quietly grind away layers of enamel from my molars, allowing my irritation to grow with each mile. This started as a good deed, but it's quickly beginning to feel like a punishment. When he starts recounting all the ways his parents have wronged him, I know I'm done. I reach back behind the seat and pull out a bottle of water from the small ice chest there. I ask him if he's thirsty. We only have a little farther to go, and surely the water will shut him up; it's a little difficult to tell some stranger way too much information if you're too busy drinking something. One can hope anyway.

He takes a water and drinks. After his third or fourth sip, the car falls into a blessed silence. I have had way too much of whatever-his-name-is today, and I think that sacred rule of not picking up hitchhikers has many more reasons than just safety. Not having to listen to some random person's life story has to be on that list, and if it's not, it definitely should be. I've added it to mine, and it's one that will be at the top when it comes to never picking up some stranger off the side of the road again.

Looking over at Joe or Jack, it appears he's dozed off for the last leg of our ride together, and I lose myself in thought with all of those possibilities resurfacing again. The knife at his side catches the light of the passing lamp posts as we move closer into town, and once again, I consider reaching for it before we get to our final destination. But once again, I think better of it. It's not going anywhere, and looking over at him, neither is he, at least not until we get to where we're going. My fears of the "what ifs" start to dissipate, and now it's only the destination that's important to me.

I almost forget he's there, or that I had picked him up, until his light snore begins to irritate me more than his talking ever did. I can't wait to get him out of my car. I've been looking forward to this retreat for a while, and I need time to work through some of this built-up stress I've been carrying around since the last time I stayed here. That seems like forever ago. I click the garage door opener and look over at Joe or Jack, or whatever his name is, and I pull into the parking space. He's off in some blissful dreamland, and I suppose he can stay there for a bit longer. He's not going to bother me anymore; his ride is over. He's made it just as far as I had promised. For now, it's time to get settled in. I'm sure he'll wake up soon enough.

About a half an hour later, he finally opens his eyes.

Looking down at him tied to the table, I smile.

Let the stress relief begin.

"Hello, Jack. Let's see if we can't work on keeping you quiet for a little while."

I enjoy the noises he tries to make through the gag I have shoved in his mouth. However, it's when his eyes catch sight of the needle and thread that I actually giggle for the first time in forever.

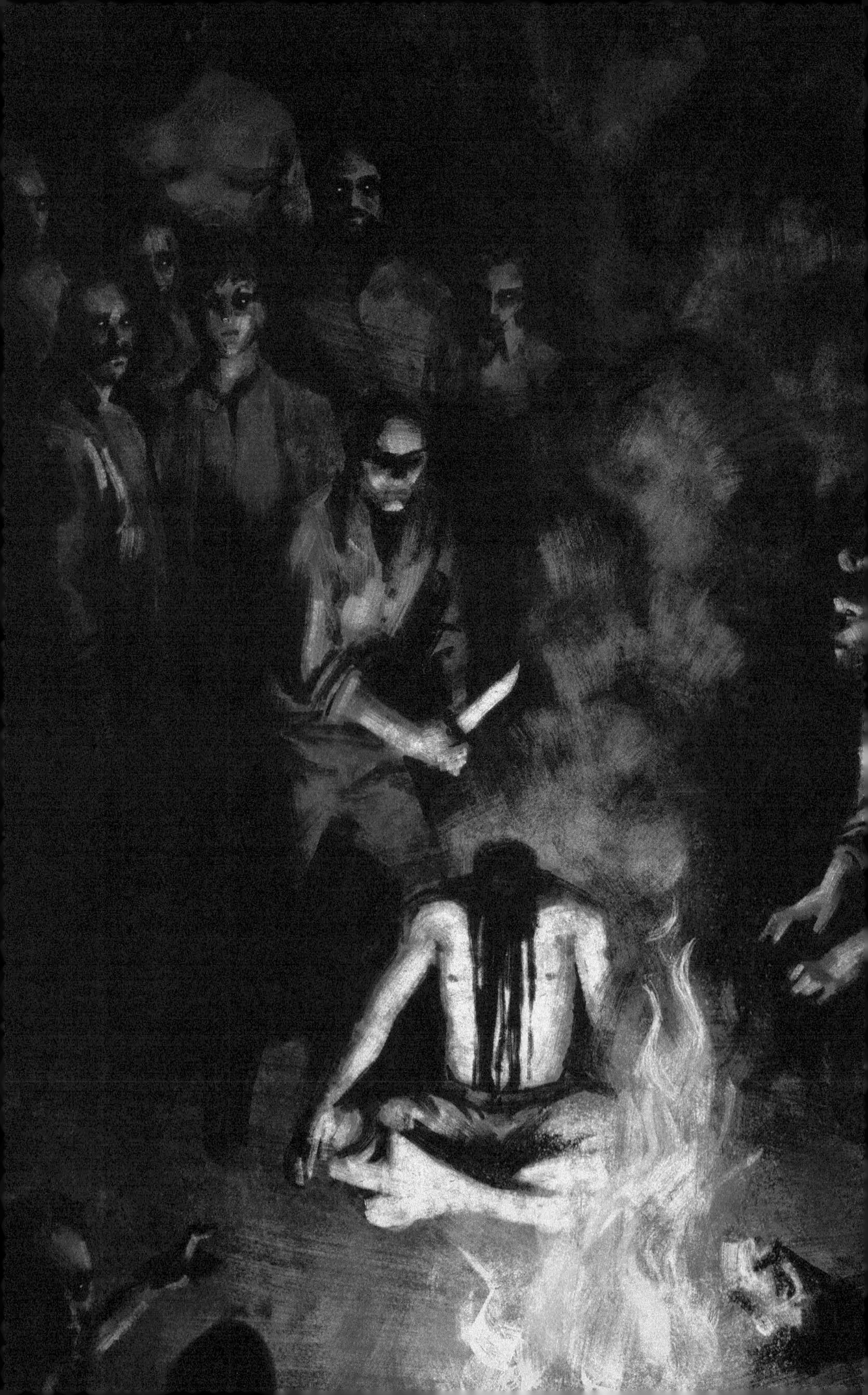

OUTSIDERS

Art by Mateus Roberts
Feature by Rob Carroll

M ateus Roberts is a Brazilian artist living in Brazil, but his style is distinctly American Gothic. Whether it's a brutal portrait of the United States during the time of the nation's westward expansion (this is my personal interpretation of *Beyond Men's Judgements*), or a more meditative piece on the existential isolation inherent to home-steaders of the time (*How the Stars Did Fall*), his work packs quite the emotional punch.

The theme I see most clearly in his work—the emotion with which I think his artwork grapples with the most—is loneliness. The subjects of his artwork, whether by choice or by force, are always set apart in some way from everything else that is both inside and even *outside* of the frame. For example, the couple in *The Turn of the Screw* are the only subjects in the frame, and yet, through clever use of perspective, the true feeling of loneliness emanates not from them, but from whatever is looking out upon them from the window in the foreground—which is also where we, the viewer, exist.

Mateus furthers these feelings of loneliness and isolation with an expert use of composition and contrast. Even when the subject isn't physically isolated, as in *Beyond Men's Judgements*, the feeling of isolation is still conjured this way. The light of the fire draws the eye to the victim and the blade that will kill him.

Pictured left: *Beyond Men's Judgements*

Mateus paints outsiders—people and places and things that have been othered by forces beyond their control. The only exception would be the malevolent *Heir Apparent*, who is no doubt an outsider by choice, and whose eyes, it's interesting to note, glow like the eyes of the mob in *Beyond Men's Judgements* (another example of men who have sacrificed their humanity by choice). These outsiders are sullen, scared, haunted, hunted, tortured, tricked and betrayed. Their worlds are dark and desolate places of midnight, shadow, and death, and only the wicked things possessed are alive with a slight orange glow. There is magic here. And mysticism.

It is for these many reasons that Mateus's work matches perfectly the tone and themes in the upcoming novella, *Linghun*, by Ai Jiang (published by Dark Matter imprint, Dark Matter INK), and why his piece, *The Fall of the House of Usher*, was chosen for the book's cover. The inverted world depicted in *The Fall of the House of Usher* is an elegant summation of how I feel whenever experiencing the otherworld of *Linghun*. And as an aside, I often wonder if all of Mateus's artworks don't exist in this same inverted realm, and that it is only via this one image that we, the viewer, are provided the glimpse needed, the perspective necessary, to know the overarching truth.

As a special treat, for the first time anywhere in print or digital, we present to you the cover reveal for *Linghun* (alongside the original, untouched artwork by Mateus) on page 39 of this issue. *Linghun* will publish April 4, 2023.

Pictured above left: *The Turn of the Screw* **Above right:** *How the Stars Did Fall*

Pictured left: *Here is Nowhere* **Top right:** *Kirie Himuro* **Bottom right:** *Heir Apparent*

Pictured above: *Lady Fujiwara*

COVER REVEAL

Mateus Roberts's artwork, *The Fall of the House of Usher*, will be on the cover of forthcoming novella LINGHUN by Ai Jiang. LINGHUN (pictured right) will be published April 4, 2023, by Dark Matter imprint, Dark Matter INK. Ai Jiang's short story "What We Look For at the Night Marktet" is included in this issue. Read the story, starting on page 115.

Pictured above: *The Fall of the House of Usher*

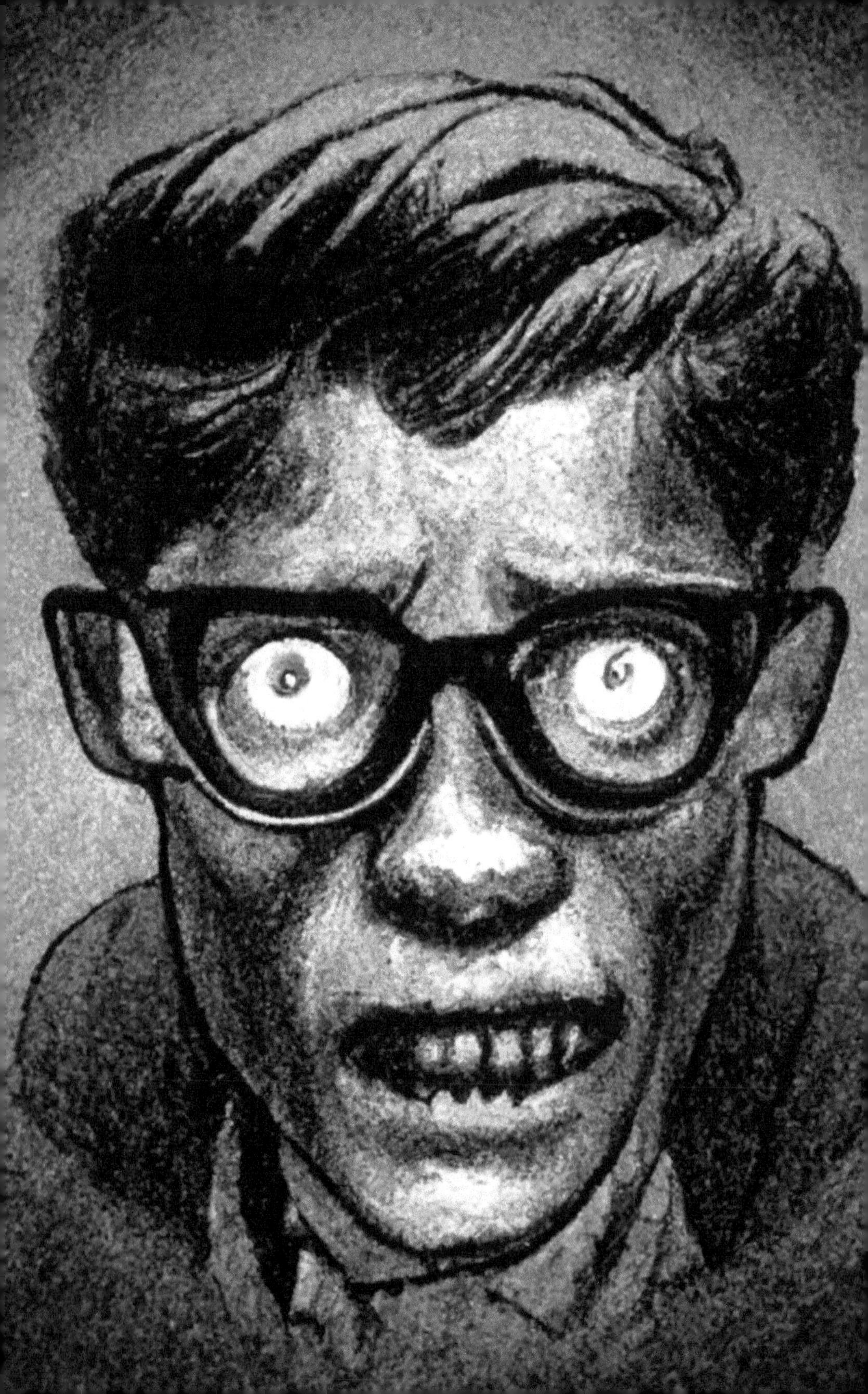

BASICALLY NORMAL

by Scotty Milder

H alsey was peeling off the college boy's eyelid when the screams erupted from up the road.

It was a woman. She sounded young, although with the way she was torturing her vocal cords it was hard to tell. Halsey hadn't heard the crunch of metal signaling a car crash. He couldn't imagine what in the hell she was on about. Whatever it was, she sure wasn't happy about it.

"Hold on, Tex," he told the college boy, and set the X-Acto knife onto the tray next to the bed. Once they made their way into his cottage, they all became "Tex" to him.

Tex went *mmmmpppf!* against the duct tape. He rattled handcuffs affixed to hooks driven crookedly into the wall. The left eyelid was already gone, leaving a blue orb gaping out from a soupy red socket. Eyes sure looked weird once you took the lids away; it made Tex look like a Muppet. The half-dissected right lid lay across the cornea like a hangnail.

Halsey had found the boy trudging up Knoles Drive, gas can in hand. The student dorm rose out of the trees to the left. A black wall of pine forest lay to the right. It was after two in the morning, so even there by the campus things were quiet. Halsey didn't usually hunt so close to home. But the defeated slump of those broad shoulders, the tired droop of the boy's red-blond hair…it was all too delicious. Halsey was pretty sure he had a good half-mile before there were any security cameras. So, he threw the car into a screeching U-turn and rolled up next to the kid. He put on his biggest shit-kicker grin and drawled *y'all need a lift?* in his thickest Rocky Mountain twang.

That was the thing about the college boys; it never occurred to them to be careful. Girls were on high alert. With them you needed a ruse, and Halsey just wasn't clever enough to come up with one. With the boys, so long as you had a set of wheels and a face that looked punchable, you were good to go. They needed to think they could lick you in a fight.

Halsey had been working at Tex for a while now. Tex didn't look much like he used to. His hair was mostly gone. Halsey read up on scalping and knew just where to cut to avoid all the arteries. The pillow was soaked in gore, but it'd be a while yet before the boy bled out.

He'd taken Tex's ears. They were now drying in Halsey's air fryer. His mom's church was having a potluck this weekend, and she was insisting Halsey take her and that he bring something. Halsey planned to make a powder from the ears and mix it with a few pounds of hamburger meat. He'd roll them into patties for Pastor McFuckstick to throw on the grill. Halsey wasn't a cannibal—or at least not the kind where he got a hard-on from it—but he giggled at the notion of all those church folk chowing on prime college boymeat.

Halsey'd also taken most of Tex's nose. The two holes in the middle of his face kept oozing blood. Halsey worried the kid would suffocate, so he shoved a couple drink straws up there to help him breathe. The last kid went way too fast. Halsey was determined to savor this one. Now Tex looked sort of like a flayed walrus, and that was just fine with Halsey. He could do without the plastic whistle of the kid's breathing, though. It was downright irritating. Next time, he decided, he'd leave the nose alone. Wasn't worth it.

He sat there, head cocked and listening, waiting for the scream. Nothing but the kid's whistle.

After a few seconds, the scream came again. Closer now. He could almost make out something which—through the thick walls of his cottage—sounded sort of like *Heeeeeaaaaameeeeeee!*

Fuck.

This time he heard it clearly: *help me!*

"Be right back," Halsey said. He stripped off the latex gloves and stuffed them into the garbage bag at the foot of the bed, next to the cut-up rags that had been the boy's NAU hoodie. He stood, stretched his neck until he felt it crack, and went into the living room.

Halsey twitched back the curtain and squinted into the dark. There were no streetlights. Halsey's cottage was on a nameless dirt track, winding toward the south flank of Humphrey's Peak. Pines pressed in, their towering forms black and jagged against the starlit night. There was a whole lot of nothing until you got down to East Appalachian Road. Up the other way was just the old Gensler place, and that had been sitting empty for five years now.

The screams came from up that way.

Presently he saw her: running down the middle of the track, shoeless and shrieking in the moonlight. An explosion of blond hair caught the silvery light and shimmered after her. It looked like someone slit her T-shirt open. It hung off her shoulders like a vest. Halsey couldn't begin to guess her age, but he didn't think she could've been more than twenty-five.

She rounded the bend and was approaching fast. "*HELP ME!*" she screamed in a voice that sounded tangled in wire. "*HEEEEEELP MEEEEEE!*"

For a traitorous moment, he was tempted to turn on the porch light and bring her in. It was curiosity more than anything; he'd put on a pot of tea and ask what happened. Then he'd decide whether to run her down to the police station or stick her in another hole out back, next to Tex. On principal, he wasn't into doing the girls the way he was the fellas. But this could be sort of like a bonus. Two for the price of one kinda deal.

But what the fuck was she doing out here, anyway? The way her shirt was cut—that sure didn't happen in no car accident. *Someone* did that. Which meant there was another person up the way demonstrating similar proclivities. And that someone would happen along directly.

Even at this distance, Halsey could tell she was a looker, which meant when she didn't show up to wherever she was supposed to show up, she'd be all over the news in about five minutes. Probably go national. This was not a headache Halsey needed.

She's gonna see the house and come here anyway, he thought sourly. And then the someone who lost her would follow. There wasn't any place else for her to go, not unless she ducked into the woods or made it down to Appalachian. And no one would figure she'd make it that far. They'd see the cottage and swing right on in. Halsey considered digging out his shotgun, just in case.

Who *was* the someone? Halsey hoped it was just a drifter or something— somebody who'd pass on and do his next business elsewhere. But he thought about the Gensler place. Hadn't he seen the "For Sale" sign out by the road go down a month back? And there was that green Grand Cherokee with the tinted windows. Halsey'd seen it creeping up the road at least three times in the last couple of weeks. It made him nervous, because the season was wrong for hiking or hunting, and there wasn't much reason else for someone to come up this way. It occurred to him it might be the FBI, keeping a watch on him.

He thought about all this as the girl pounded past, still screaming. She never even gave the cottage a glance.

And sure enough, as the girl's shrieks faded in one direction, he heard the growl of an engine coming from the other. Headlights splashed across trees, knocking loose every whorl and crag. He couldn't quite make out the vehicle, but it was dark and hulking and sure as shit could've been a Grand Cherokee.

Looked like Halsey had new neighbor.

A *particular sort* of neighbor.

Halsey let the curtain drop and went back into the bedroom. The smell of blood, fat, and feces was hot and meaty. Halsey felt his own blood rush to engorge his member. *Goddamn.* Too bad he was going to have to cut his evening short. Halsey had meant to really stretch this one out past the breaking point. But with these new developments, he didn't think he had the time. Someone was likely to be coming around looking for the girl, and he didn't want to be hip-deep in a grave when they did.

Tex's lidless eyes rolled toward him. He *mmmph*ed and rattled the handcuffs. Blood and mucus bubbled around the straws.

Halsey picked up the X-Acto knife

"Y'all sure are spirited, Tex," he said, thinking it never hurt to drop a word or two of encouragement. "But we got us a little problem."

Morning came cool and tentative, like the sun itself was scared to see what Halsey was up to.

By the time he stumbled back inside—the bad disc in his back screaming, his pants caked with mud, and his arms smeared with gore to the wrist—it was almost time for that morning news show out of Phoenix. He didn't much care for the lady host. She was blonde and had big teeth and laughed a lot at nothing. The fella she sat with had a face that was once handsome but was now starting to sag in all the wrong places.

The one Halsey watched for was the weather kid. He was tall and strapping, with sculpted Ken Doll hair. He looked fresh scrubbed and like maybe he graduated from weather school or whatever two weeks ago. When he smiled, it was like y'all were sharing an inside joke. More than once, Halsey thought about taking the drive down to Phoenix, maybe tracking the kid down. It couldn't be too hard; not like the kid was the fucking pope or some shit. Halsey'd sure like to chain him up on that mattress and call him Tex.

It was still a few minutes early, though, so Halsey turned on the coffee pot and staggered into the shower. The water was so hot it was near scalding, which was exactly what Halsey needed to pound out that growing knot in his lower back.

He scrubbed the viscera from his arms and face, watched it wash down the mold-speckled drain. Halsey wondered how long it would take for those stray filaments of DNA to work their way into the Colorado River.

The water stripped off the stench as well. The smell was so pungent it made Halsey's eyes water. He then dragged the corpse outside to where he'd already dug the hole.

He shut the water off and grabbed the least-dirty towel from the floor.

Minutes later, he carried a steaming mug into the living room and snapped on the TV. He didn't expect there to be any news about the girl—not yet— so he was shocked to see a haggard-looking young lady doing a stand-up in front of what looked like the Methodist church, right down by the East Appalachian turnoff. Crime-scene tape flapped behind her.

The coffee went cold as Halsey watched, mouth agape. The girl wasn't a girl at all; her name was Sheila Flake, and she was a thirty-five-year-old mother of two. They said this over and over again. There was a studio shot of Sheila smiling behind what he assumed were fake pearls. Seems someone was out walking their dog and found her head in the church parking lot. No word on the rest of the body.

No mention of Tex yet, not that Halsey expected there to be. With the college boys, it generally took a week or more before anyone thought to report them missing.

Sheila Flake's goddamned head was the story of the day. Hell, it was probably gonna be the story of the year. They never even cut to the weather kid.

Right there, in the church parking lot.

At the bottom of the turn.

Halsey thought of himself as a basically normal guy with a hobby he knew others would find unseemly. He prided himself on being careful. Last night notwithstanding, he never trolled around Flagstaff or even northern Arizona. All Halsey's boys came from down south, around Phoenix or Tucson, and once up the way in Utah.

And he sure as shit never left a goddamned *head* right at the mouth of the road. There were only two houses up this way. One of them was Halsey's.

He was gonna have to pay his new neighbor a visit. He needed to explain the way things worked around here.

Halsey decided to walk. His arms and back were screaming from his late-night exertions, but the Gensler place was only a half-mile up, and the going wasn't all that steep until you got to the last bend. It seemed to him that if his new neighbor was similarly paranoid and heard an engine approaching, he might batten down the hatches. Best to show up like the welcome wagon, and then just spring it on him: *I don't care what you're up to, but y'all'er gonna need to be a lot more careful if we're gonna get along.*

His great granddaddy had an old revolver he'd nicked off a dead German during WW1. Halsey wasn't too fond of guns himself, but he figured— considering the way this conversation was apt to go—he'd best be carrying something. So, he dug the pistol out of the old shoe box on his closet shelf, checked the loads, and shoved it into the back of his jeans. He had no idea whether the cartridges would even fire. But at least the fucking thing looked mean.

By the time he rounded that last bend, he was regretting leaving the truck behind. Sweat poured out of him in a rank, oily sheen. Even the shade provided by the pines couldn't dampen the heat. And now it wasn't just his back and arms that were killing him, but his whole goddamned body. It felt like someone was driving augur bits into his hip bones.

But he came around the bend and there was the Gensler place, pushing out of the trees like a canker. It was a ranch-style house, the shingles painted a deep brown to blend with the pines. It looked more dilapidated than Halsey remembered; the roof sagged, and the black windows gaped out at the road like the sad eyes of a stupid dog. The arched double door was like the yawing grimace of a hinged-open jawbone. But sure enough, there was the green Grand Cherokee sitting at the top of the gravel drive.

As Halsey turned off the road and stepped onto the property, he was thinking about how he was going to broach the subject. Did he just come out and say it—*look, I got the same general recreational interests as you*—or did he beat around the bush a little? Probe delicately, like a dentist with an impacted molar? Or come on like a steam engine? He supposed he'd figure it out once he got the measure of the fella.

It never occurred to him to look down. The last conscious thought he had was an awareness of the slight tug at his left ankle. He never heard the blast. The shotgun was wedged into the armpit of a pine, aimed roughly at chest level—or it would've been for a slightly taller man. As it was, the slug pulped Halsey's skull like a sledgehammer swung against a rotten pumpkin. Blood, brains, and puzzle-piece chunks of bone scattered wetly across the gravel. The right eye jellied immediately, and the left hurled itself off into the trees, trailing a rope of viscera like a comet's tail.

Halsey's legs kept moving for half-a-second, not yet aware that he was dead. Then they crumpled, pitching the now functionally headless corpse to the gravel.

Silence fell, cut only by the far-off shriek of a jay.

Seconds passed.

Then the double doors swung open.

A few hours later, someone reported a column of black smoke rising above the pines on that unnamed county road spiking north off East Appalachian. The Flagstaff fire department went screaming up there, sirens blaring, desperate to get there before the whole forest and half the city went up in flames.

The next morning it was reported that a cottage owned by one Halsey Ryan, forty-eight, had burned flat. Once the flames were extinguished, authorities discovered Mr. Ryan's burnt body in the wreckage. It appeared he'd lit the fire and then shot himself in the head.

They also found the headless body of a woman in the cottage. Reporters breathlessly speculated that this was, in fact, Sheila Flake, although they were careful to say that confirmation was still forthcoming.

Cadaver dogs found the bodies of five others buried in various spots behind the cottage. The most recent appeared to be that of NAU engineering student Jeffrey Turner, twenty-one, who'd been reported missing by his roommate just the day before.

It took the papers one more day to come up with a name: *The Flagstaff Flayer.*

The story remained alive for another week, but without a perp walk or a trial, there wasn't much else to report. The police closed the case, the reporters moved onto other things, and everything returned to normal.

Basically.

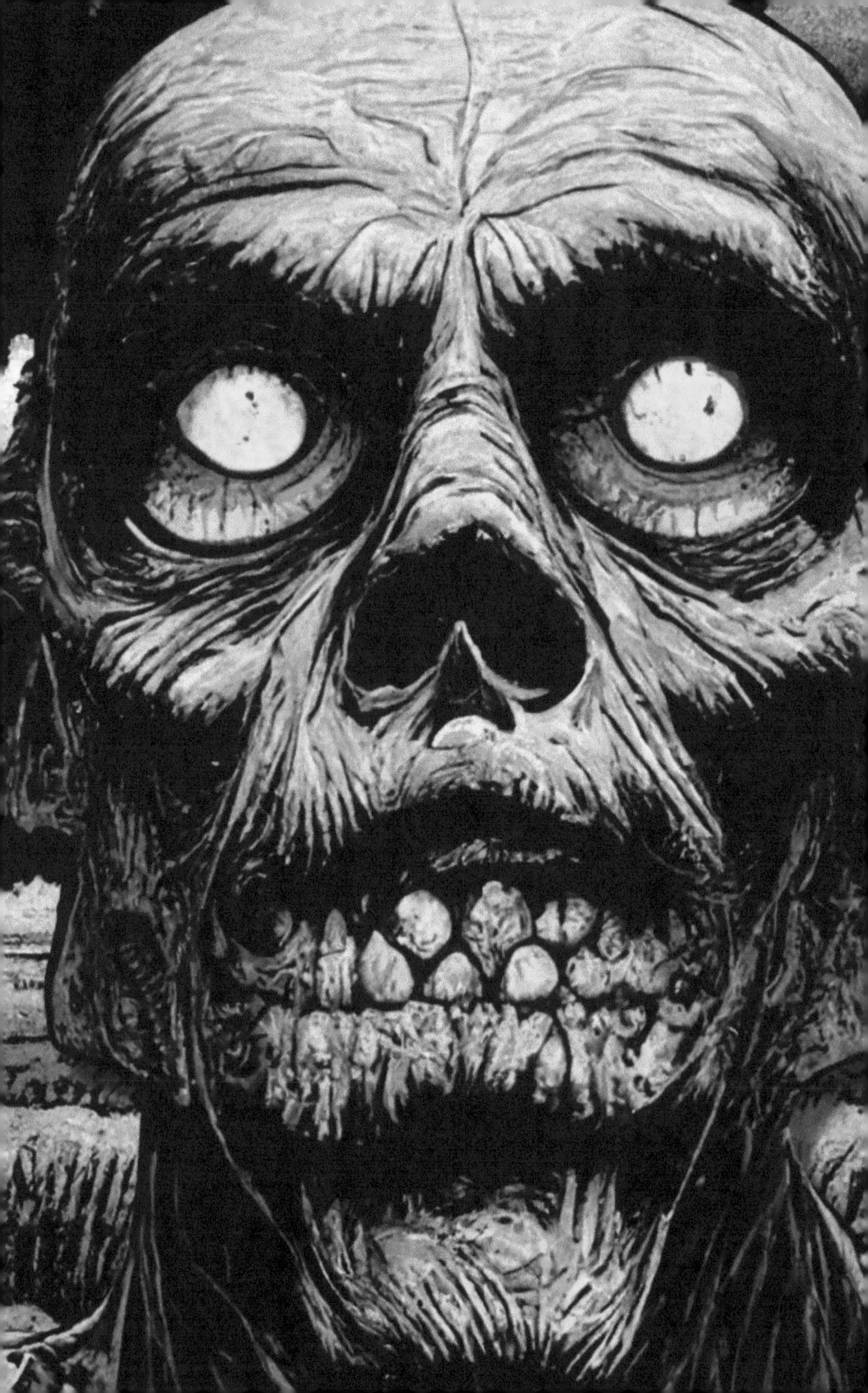

STORM CELLAR

by Jen Marshall

I n this town, we believe in monsters. There was a time when I would have excluded myself from that statement. Not anymore. See, my buddy Dale's oldest boy trapped a monster in a storm cellar. That's what I'll believe until the day I die.

Now, this all happened years ago, back when so many folks around here were having trouble with their deer blinds and hunting stands. There was something in the woods at night, trashing everything when nobody was around.

After several incidents, Dale bought himself a night-vision, motion-activated trail cam and mounted it on his tree stand. It got smashed to pieces a few nights later, but not before it took one blurry photograph. It was hard to see much in that hazy image, but what little was visible was enough to make a man feel weak.

A bony arm reached toward the camera, the skin powdery and pale like you'd find on a dog with mange. The face was in shadow except for a single eye and thin lips pulled back in an animal snarl. That eye was the worst part. It looked black and distorted because of the night-vision setting, but there was an intelligence there that didn't belong to any local wildlife. That photo was all the proof we needed. It was a monster, plain and simple.

Now, before you dismiss us as gullible rednecks, there's one thing you need to understand. In this part of the country, we don't just live to hunt. We hunt to live. Messing with another man's hunting blinds is a crime we can't abide, and destroying them, well that's something we simply can't comprehend. A monster was the only explanation we could live with. Anything else was inconceivable.

The hardware store over on Main Street, that's my place. There's typically a steady stream of folks coming and going, trading gossip and fishing stories and whatnot. I like to think they stop in for my company. More likely it's the free coffee and the fact that it's the only business in town still open besides the Grocery & Drug and a handful of bars. In any case, Dale's oldest boy was always dropping by to shoot the shit with my customers, and that's how he wound up leaning on my counter one day, bragging about how he'd captured the beast that was wrecking everyone's hunting blinds.

"I climbed up to my old man's deer stand, you know the one over by Route Y and 44? So, I waited up there until dark, then I guess I fell asleep, because the next thing I knew there was rustling and footsteps down below. I took a few shots in that direction, but I must've missed because after that I heard something crashing through the underbrush like it was running away—"

"Hold up," I said. "You shot at something you couldn't see?"

"Hell yeah, I shot at it. It's a monster. Didn't you see the dang picture? Anyways, I jumped down and chased that varmint through the woods and clear across the field toward the abandoned houses out there. You know the ones?"

I knew the ones. Everyone in town knew them. Vacant buildings are everywhere in this part of the county ever since the mill shut down, most of them crumbling like the American Dream. The houses out by Route Y, though, they were old school, built strong and hardy to withstand the harsh weather we're famous for here. Each one was equipped with a backyard storm cellar, the kind with double doors lying on the ground at a slight incline, like the ones in that *Wizard of Oz* movie.

Folks like us know precisely what to do when the sky turns storm-green, and the air gets thick and stagnant. We run out to the yard with a radio, a flashlight, and whatever pets we can get our hands on. The first person to the cellar flings open the doors, and the last one down the steps slams them shut behind him.

It was in one of those storm cellars where Dale's boy claimed he'd trapped the monster. He said he'd shoved an old board through both handles to secure the doors from the outside. He went on and on, boasting about how he'd done the community a valuable service.

"Son, you know better than that," I said. "No self-respecting hunter traps something, then leaves it to die. I don't care what it is; you either kill it or you let it go. That's all there is to it."

"What am I supposed to do? Open the doors and say, 'pleased to meet you and sorry for the trouble.' Maybe I should douse myself in BBQ sauce while I'm at it, make sure whatever's in there enjoys its meal."

"Sounds like quite a predicament. The quicker you solve it the better, because you're not welcome in my store until you do."

Dale's boy flapped around some, carrying on about how I should be thanking him instead of busting his chops. But what's right is right, and he knew arguing would get him nowhere. He gave me a dirty look on his way out.

That boy was an idiot. He engaged in all the trashiest rural American pastimes: dynamite fishing, deer shining, cow tipping, petty vandalism. Doing that crap made him a clichéd small-town loser; doing it wrong made him an idiot. He'd screwed up his arm setting off explosives at the lake a few years prior, and another time, the sheriff had to disentangle him from a low-voltage electric fence surrounding a cow pasture. One winter, he backed his truck into an oversized papier-mâché shoe that was part of a local art installation, yet another failed attempt at downtown revitalization. It somehow got hooked to his bumper, and he dragged that giant shoe around town for days without realizing it until the police pulled him over. Like I said, he was an idiot.

Truth be told, all Dale's boys had problems. The middle son was a notorious shoplifter as a kid. He was constantly pocketing candy from my store, looking so hungry that half the time I pretended not to notice. Eventually he progressed to burglarizing houses and stealing cars. Last I heard, he was serving time for a drug-related offense.

Dale's youngest son, now he was the one I've always had a soft spot for. He never made a single sound, not from the day he was born. He could hear fine, but he didn't speak, laugh, or cry, not once. Doctors gave a diagnosis, but Dale could never remember what it was. The kid always wore a red baseball cap. Never took it off, no matter if he was chopping wood or sitting in church. Boy loved his hat.

He never much cared for hunting or fishing though, and when he got older, he flat-out refused to touch a gun. He wrote poems; beautiful things that made my soul ache for something I didn't even know I was missing. But you can't be a man like that in a town like this. The shame of it nearly destroyed Dale.

All those boys ever wanted was their father's approval, but he never taught them how to earn it. Instead, he sat in the bar and complained how he'd been cursed with a halfwit, a criminal, and a sissy mute instead of the offspring he deserved. Those reputations clung to his boys like the stench of skunk on a hunting dog. God damn this town. I don't know how anybody survives it.

Well, about a week had passed before I noticed that Dale's oldest boy hadn't made his way back to my store yet. He was constantly going off hunting or prowling or God knows what, so nobody in town thought a thing of it. I guessed he was still in a huff because I'd treated him like a child, maybe roughed his feelings a bit. I didn't give a rat's ass about that, as long as he'd taken care of his business in the cellar. No creature deserves to die like that, alone and afraid in a dark hole in the earth.

It took a bit longer for real worry to set in, and then I figured I ought to check on the situation myself. Those old houses were a decent distance from Main Street, but I didn't care to take my truck, not with all the potholes and washboard road out there. Besides, I prefer walking. It sets me to thinking, which ordinarily I appreciate. This time, though, my mind filled with endless questions, relentless and stinging like sand in the wind, making each step a misery.

What if the cellar doors were open? What were the implications of that, considering that the boy appeared to be missing? What if I found the doors still blocked shut? Should I open them myself? Or should I drag Dale's son back there and force him to take responsibility?

That damn fool. Everyone knows you don't trap something you can't kill or set loose.

As soon as I arrived at the edge of the woods, I could see him lying on top of that storm cellar, calm as you please. I hollered to him from across the field and when he didn't move, I knew he was dead. It was like how you can sense a house is empty just by setting foot in the door. It's easy to tell when there's no one home.

The smell of decay overwhelmed me as I got closer, and I realized I'd been mistaken about him being peaceful. His eyes and mouth were wide open, and he looked terrified, as though the last thing he'd seen was the devil himself. The boy's wrist was caught in the thin crack where the doors came together, mangled and skinned to the bone from his attempts to pull it out. He'd stuffed his rifle through the two handles to keep the doors shut. The wooden board he'd used previously for that purpose lay on the ground a few feet away.

Straight off, I vomited. After that, I sat down in the grass and bawled. I had a pretty good notion of what had happened to Dale's oldest son. He'd pulled the board out of the door handles to look inside and then chucked it off to the side. Something had transpired then that scared him bad enough to change his mind about opening the doors. Panicking, he'd slid his rifle through the handles to secure them, but he couldn't take it out again because whatever was in the cellar must have been pushing at the doors from the inside, trying to escape. I don't know how he managed to get his arm caught, but his aforementioned fish-bombing injuries had probably contributed to it.

I imagined him sitting there with his wrist all mashed and broken, yelling until his voice gave out, pondering his situation. He must have been in terrible pain, which likely further hindered his already limited capacity for problem solving. He couldn't shoot through the doors because he was using his gun to keep them closed. And with his jacked-up arm, attempting a quick grab and point was too risky. He must have guessed that whatever was inside would get him first.

It's hard to know what finally killed him. I'd wager it was a combination of blood loss and shock. One thing was certain: he died scared. Poor bastard was afraid to open those doors and face whatever he'd trapped; afraid of what would happen if he didn't; afraid of dying; afraid of living and explaining to his father what his stupidity had wrought. It was a bad death. An idiot's death.

If you ask me, the saddest part was that he did it for Dale. He was nearly a grown man and he'd never stopped trying to impress his daddy. It made me sick. My head felt like it was full of flies and only one clear thought emerged from the buzzing. I couldn't let Dale see his son like that.

So, I set to sawing at his wrist with my hunting knife. When I got to the bone, I snapped it with my boot, and whatever was left of his hand dropped into the cellar with a distant wet thud. I slid the rifle out from under the handles and replaced it with the wooden board. Then I dragged that young man away from the trap he'd made for himself.

Pointless as it was, I put my ear against the doors and listened to the cold silence inside. Whatever creature was in there had surely died long ago, probably with the taste of Dale's oldest boy's blood on its tongue.

After making sure the body was decent and resting comfortably, I headed straight to Dale's house, aiming to tell him the bad news before he heard it from somebody else. He opened the door with a smile, talking nonstop about how nobody was tampering with the hunting stands anymore, not since his boys had intervened.

"I reckon they shot the son-of-a-bitch that was causing the trouble, and now they're off carousing and raising hell together, having a fine old time," Dale said.

I felt a hint of fear then, like a tickle in the back of my throat. I coughed as he let me into his house.

"Both boys?"

"Yep. I know I'm always saying how they ain't nothing but a moron and a pansy, but turns out they've got something of their old man in them after all."

"How long have they been gone?"

"Two weeks, give or take. Hell if I know. I ain't their keeper. All I know is they took off together, and they'll come back when they're good and ready."

He laughed and pushed his hat back, and I noticed he wasn't wearing his regular green John Deere. It was a ratty old red baseball cap.

"Darnedest thing," he said when I inquired about it. "I found it on the ground a few paces from my deer stand. Boy must have accidentally dropped it before skipping town. I figured I'd keep it safe for him until he gets back."

Dale's youngest boy would never have left that red hat behind, not under any circumstances. Anyone who's ever met him would vouch for that. I almost said as much to Dale, but that itch of fear I'd felt earlier rose up and choked me and I couldn't get a word out. Instead, I listened to my buddy since the third grade crowing about his sons like they were heroes. I understood then that there was only one course of action: keep my damn mouth shut.

Go ahead and throw stones if you think you could have done better. Maybe you're the type of person who would have told Dale exactly what you'd found lying on those cellar doors. Maybe you'd have led him back there so he could see for himself. Hell, if you're strong enough to watch your friend's heart collapse and spill out his newfound pride in his sons onto a stained and cigarette-burned carpet, then I salute you.

As for me, I buried Dale's oldest boy with his gun and his dignity in an unmarked grave in the woods. Then I went home to live the rest of my life as best I could. I never did look inside that storm cellar.

Some folks might drive themselves crazy wondering what was in there. They might obsessively study a copy of that old trail cam picture and speculate on all the unthinkable possibilities. Some folks might even wake up screaming night after night, soaked in sweat and crying like a baby, trying to remember if they'd really heard the sound of fingernails weakly scratching on the underside of a cold metal door, or if that was only the figment of a dream.

Not me. In this town, we believe in monsters. So, I never have to wonder. My buddy Dale's oldest boy trapped a monster in a storm cellar. That's what I'll believe until the day I die.

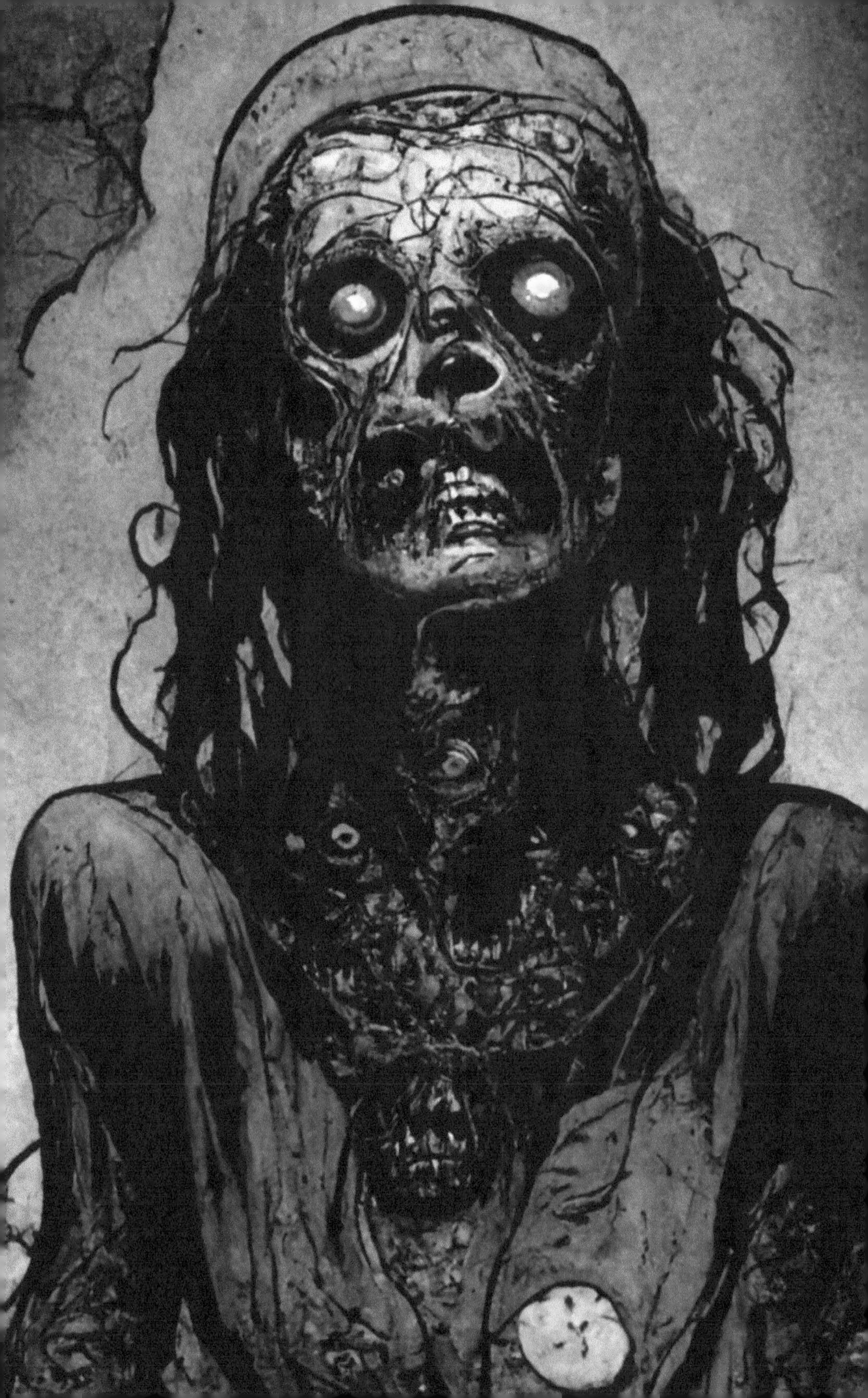

SHOCK

by Casey Masterson

The man only known as Red was greeted with a human doll and muffled screams from upstairs. Red had met his host, Richard (username *rhannedy75*), on Craigslist. The outdated site was about as close to the black market as the average person could venture. With shoppers diverted to Amazon and (less commonly) eBay, those with questionable wares ranging from hookers to organs to willing victims of crime took over, waiting for buyers to stumble upon their advertised services. Red (username *j4n6QhR4Txy2*), offered "medical services, pending payment." He didn't ask when Richard offered him money, he didn't ask when he had to drive out into The-Land-With-No-Reception, and he didn't ask about the smell of roadkill when the bespectacled man opened the door. But what he saw what awaited him, he couldn't hold his tongue.

"What the *fuck* is that?"

"*Shh!* She can hear you." Richard pushed up his horn-rimmed glasses and walked toward the couch, standing behind the doll. "This is my wife, Rebecca."

Red had seen people shot, people iced in a tub with their kidneys out, but never anything like what Richard called "Rebecca." The smell of moldy cold cuts was proof of her authenticity, but nothing screamed human about her. Her eyes were glass. Eye shadow and eyeliner were smudged and poorly applied. Her skin looked plastic, not in the way corpses in funeral homes do, but in a way that made her face look covered in plaster, eyes bulging out like a goldfish. Her body was wrapped in rags, and a blanket was thrown over her lap.

"What did you *do* to her?"

"Nothing." Richard leaned down to kiss Rebecca's head. The scalp of hair moved, clearly unattached. It might have looked more realistic if he put a mop or corn husks on her head. "You should have seen her before."

Red shook his head. "Look, man, her organs aren't going to be any good."

Richard cocked his head to the side, confused. His blue eyes reminded Red of the frozen corpses found up on Mount Everest: cold, gone from this world. "You aren't here for Rebecca," he replied.

The noise from upstairs continued.

"I dunno, man. This don't feel right."

"Are you quitting?" Richard frowned. "You said you were accustomed to these kinds of operations."

"Yeah, but this shit's *fucked.*"

Richard didn't say anything. He clucked his tongue once, twice, three times. "I'll pay you double."

"You're bluffing."

Richard closed the distance between them. Red shifted his weight back, moving a leg with it, but an attack never came. Instead, his employer fell to his knees, hands grasping at his ankles, tugging at the hem. "Please, I'm begging you. You'll get all the money you want, all of it and more, just please, *please,* you have to trust me."

Usually when Red saw people beg, it was because he was holding a gun to their head, or a knife to their neck. But now, without the aid of either, he watched Richard's shoulders rise and fall, listened to his breath catch in his throat. Richard's tears fell on Red's sneakers, and Red ripped his foot away. He thought about kicking the man, but stopped himself before he ruined the deal.

Easy money. Just do what the sick fuck wants and take the cash.

"What do you want from her?" Red motioned with his head to the staircase and to the sound upstairs. The sound became a thump, followed by a low wail.

"Her brain. Everything else is yours."

"Man, murder wasn't a part of this deal!"

"No, you don't understand!" Richard scrambled to his feet. He wiped the tears from his eyes and gripped Red's shoulders. "I'm not *killing* her. She'll live again, she'll live through Rebecca. See, Rebecca had brain cancer. She doesn't have a brain now, but if she had one… I've read that electricity can recharge muscles, make them move again. If you read *Frankenstein* or… or… You'll see! She won't die, you'll see."

"You aren't paying me enough for this shit."

"You know how much these organs sell for separately, right? Imagine how much you can make from *all of them*." Richard gripped Red's shoulders tighter. "How much would an organ like the heart go for, huh? Or *both* kidneys?"

Red shoved him away, but he had to admit, the man's pitch got him thinking. A kidney went for about $25,000. But a heart? He'd seen those go for a hundred grand. It wouldn't take much to kill the woman upstairs, and the payout would be huge.

Let the weirdo have his brain, Red thought. *I'm gonna get paid.*

"You got ice?"

"I went and bought a few bags this morning. I thought you might–"

"Good. Go set up the bathtub. I'll take care of the rest."

Along the staircase wall were pictures of Richard and his wife. Rebecca, in life, had olive skin and blonde hair that fell in rivers over her shoulders. Sometimes she wore it in French braids. As Red ascended, the pictures of Rebecca changed. First, her hair was cut shorter, then later, her head was wrapped in a scarf.

Every door upstairs was closed, but the sounds of terror were hard to misplace. He walked past two doors on his right in favor of the last door on his left. Red twisted the knob and entered.

Oh fuck.

His intended victim was tied to the bedpost by her wrists. Her body hung off one side, and her bare feet were kicking desperately against the carpet. Her heels were bleeding from the constant friction, and it appeared as though her right shoulder was badly dislocated, the bone protruding at an odd angle. A filthy rag was stuffed inside her mouth.

As Red approached, her kicks became more furious. She was exhausted and terrified, a dangerous combination, kicks thrown at random with no goal in mind other than survival. She pulled on her restraints, which exacerbated her injury and made her muffled shrieks louder.

Red approached with his hands outstretched. Her feet met his hands once, twice, as he did his best to catch them, like a bear fishing for river salmon. As soon as Red caught one of her feet, he yanked. He wanted to get the woman to the ground and eliminate her leverage, but she rolled to her side in an evasive maneuver right as Red moved to climb on top of her.

The easiest way is to break her neck. Just one quick twist and she's gone.

Red gripped her cheeks. Her legs flailed behind him, and tears and snot ran down her cheeks. She begged with her eyes for mercy even as they began to bulge from their sockets. Red gripped harder and then quickly twisted her neck violently in an attempt to snap it. He twisted with no luck. And then he twisted again.

Why won't she die?

His victim, still very much alive, tried once more to escape, but she didn't have the strength to succeed.

Red grabbed her head again and—

"Don't!" It was Richard. He was standing in the doorway, where he had dropped the bag of ice to the floor.

At the sight of him, the tied-up woman peed herself in fear.

"You might damage the brain stem."

"Then why don't you do it yourself?" Red snapped.

Richard clucked his tongue. "Why don't you go fill up the bathtub? It's right across the hall."

"Whatever you say," Red replied. He grabbed the bag of ice from the floor on his way out.

As he left the room, he heard Richard humming a familiar tune, though the name of the song escaped him. He threw open the bathroom door, drew back the shower curtain, threw the Dove 2-in-1 shampoo on the ground, and poured the ice into the tub. The sound of crushed ice being dumped muted the sounds of the woman's screams in the other room, which rose in crescendo and then fell silent.

"...lucky I'm in love with my best friend, dah-da da dah-dah de da da..."

Richard entered the bathroom with the woman slumped over his shoulder. His blue button-up was stained crimson.

Red couldn't quite tell what Richard had done to finish her off. There was blood—so much blood—but no visible wounds.

Her chest rose and fell.

"She's still breathing," Red said with surprise.

"It'll give you a bit longer with the organs, won't it?"

Red sighed. "Go get the coolers from my truck."

Richard nodded, turning on his heel. "...lucky I'm in love in every way, lucky to have stayed where we have stayed..."

Red took the brain out last.

Richard looked on in chastised silence (he'd been told to shut up on more than one occasion), standing with hands in his pockets, back pressed against the wall, eyes fixed in glassy reverie. Occasionally, he would hum, but he would quickly stop at the first sign of Red tensing up.

Each organ went one after the other into the coolers. Blood dripped down the sides.

Red came to the brain and paused before proceeding. He looked over his shoulder at Richard. "When is this…this surgery of yours happening?"

"As soon as humanly possible."

Red set his jaw and slid his tongue over his teeth. He had sewn the woman back up where he could. The chest was impossible to fix, considering he had to go in with garden shears to crack her ribs, and with the skull…well, he just placed the top back on like the lid to a jar. He put the brain in a bowl of ice and handed it to his benefactor.

Richard held the bowl and regarded the brain with reverence.

"I…I can't thank you enough for this."

"Don't mention it."

"I mean it, I–"

"I mean it, too. Don't mention it. *Ever.*"

"Oh. Gotcha." Richard smiled sheepishly. "Want to make an extra thousand?"

"I'm not getting rid of the body for you." The tub was quite literally a bloodbath, and it would take more than bleach to sanitize the room. "Do that shit yourself."

"No, no, I just…Well, I could use some help with Rebecca's procedure." Richard pinched the frame of his glasses with his thumb and middle finger and adjusted them on his face. "I understand if I've used too much of your time already. I'm sure you're a busy man."

No way I'm sticking around for this shitshow.

"I'll pass."

"Please? I just, well, I'm not sure I can lift the battery. I'm pretty sure it weighs as much as I do."

"And what are you going to do with this battery, huh? Attach it to her and watch her fry?"

"Something like that. But she won't fry. You'll see. I've prepped her body. She looks better than before."

Red pressed his lips together. "An extra thousand?"

"Yes, yes." Richard was already out the bathroom door, trotting down the stairs.

Red followed.

"The battery's in the shed. Just go out the front, you'll see it in the yard," Richard took the blanket from Rebecca's lap and threw it over the back of the couch. He took her in his arms and eased her onto her back. He kneeled next to the couch, holding her hand in his, whispering God-knows-what to her.

Fucking creep.

Once alone outside, Red debated leaving, but decided against it. Today was like a car accident and he couldn't bring himself to look away. He lugged the battery and some jumper cables in from the shed, as instructed.

Back inside, Rebecca's wig of hair lay on the ground. Her skull was empty.

"Where'd her brain go?" Red asked. He set the battery down.

"They took it out when she was embalmed," Richard replied. He let go of Rebecca's hand. "You know, the Egyptians used to pull the brain out from the nose."

"Gross." Red plugged the battery into the nearest outlet. "Look, man, this ain't gonna work."

"It worked in *Frankenstein*." Richard connected a jumper cable to the battery, kissed his wife's brow, hesitated, then clamped the cable to her arm. At first, there was a sudden jolt. Then smoke. Then flames. The fabric wrapping her arms, legs, everywhere, was instantly alight. Rebecca's cheap makeup melted from her face.

Richard didn't scream, but Red noticed every ounce of terror prepare to leap from his throat. Red yanked the plug from the outlet, but the damage was already done. The fire spread to the couch, then to the blanket draped across the back. Richard dashed from the room. As Red stomped out the gathering flames, Richard returned with a fire extinguisher. The fire was stopped with a cloud of CO_2.

Rebecca's corpse was destroyed. One glass eye had burst, and with the rags burned away, Red could now see bone. A strange liquid seeped into the couch.

"What have I done?" Richard whispered. He reached an arm out toward Rebecca but withdrew it immediately. "My God, what have I done?"

"Hate to say I told you so." Red crossed his arms over his chest.

Richard didn't move, didn't turn to sneer at him. His shoulders slumped. "I...I killed that girl upstairs, didn't I? She's really gone."

"Yeah."

Red leaned down and clapped Richard on the shoulder. "I'm out of here, man. Good luck with all this."

"I can bring Julia back," Richard mumbled.

"What?"

"Julia, the girl from upstairs, I can bring her back. I just need to lower the wattage, maybe even get a better conductor…" Richard began to laugh, then stopped. He turned to Red.

"How would you like to make an extra ten grand?"

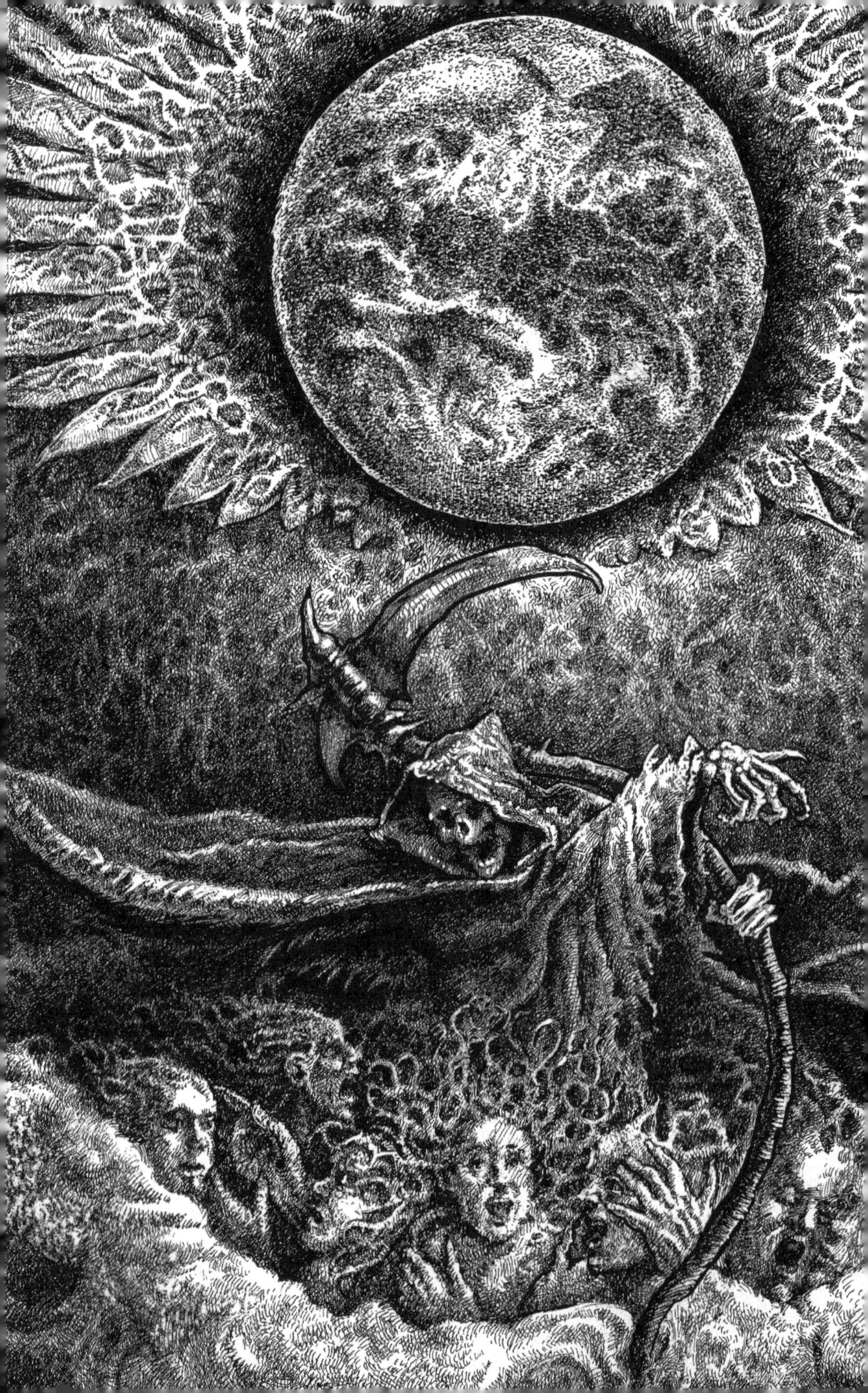

NINE CIRCLES

Art by Zach Horvath
Introduction by Rob Carroll

I want to start this art feature with an extended quotation from my interview with Zach Horvath, the artist whose work is featured here, because I believe it deserves the space. Some things are just better presented uncut. Here it is:

"I think it's fascinating how our familiarity with people and places influences our perception of them," Zach tells me. "I struggled with heroin addiction for nearly a decade, and in the last two years of my run, I was homeless and sleeping under bridges and in abandoned parking lots. Streets and neighborhoods that I once thought of as being dangerous and scary became normal fixtures in my life, and I became another addition to the scenery. Though that period was pretty rough, I came to appreciate things I would have been afraid to explore otherwise. The ingenuity and creativity of the human spirit is still very much alive in even the most dismal circumstances."

Even before our interview, I was struck by the dark romantic quality of Zach's work. The American Romantic Movement, for which the dark romantics were a part, included members Edgar Allan Poe, Nathanial Hawthorne, Herman Melville, and Emily Dickinson, and focused on themes of human fallibility, self-destruction, judgment, punishment, guilt, and sin. After my interview with Zach, I was struck by how much his real life

Pictured left: *Reaper*

struggles align with the struggles explored by the dark romantics, and I no longer wondered how it came to be that his work feels so familiar to the bygone movement.

Zach's stated influences are wide-ranging and include a variety of styles, from Renaissance painter Leonardo da Vinci to comic book greats like Frank Miller, Todd McFarlane, and Jean Giraud (aka Moebius). But the influence that stuck out to me the most was French artist, Gustave Doré.

Doré illustrated six books during his career: The Bible, John Milton's *Paradise Lost*, Dante Alighieri's *The Divine Comedy*, *Don Quixote* by Miguel de Cervantes, William Shakespeare's *The Tempest*, and *The Raven* by Edgar Allan

Pictured top: *Crispy* **Bottom left:** *Suit* **Bottom right:** *The Creator and the Vampire*

Pictured top: *Towers*   **Bottom:** *The Raven*

Poe. Three of these works are Biblical in nature, one is the actual Bible, one is about a Christian knight-errant, and the other is about a winged messenger from the underworld. Zach's work features messengers from the underworld, trips through the nine circles of Hell, and pilgrims seeking counsel with a triumvirate of Biblically accurate angels.

Gustave Doré is one of my favorite artists of all time, so I take great pleasure in seeing a young artist carry on Doré's rich tradition, not just in style, but in theme and subject matter as well.

There is a forgotten book of symbols being resurrected by a number of modern artists today, and Zach is certainly among their ranks.

Pictured above: *Cherubim*

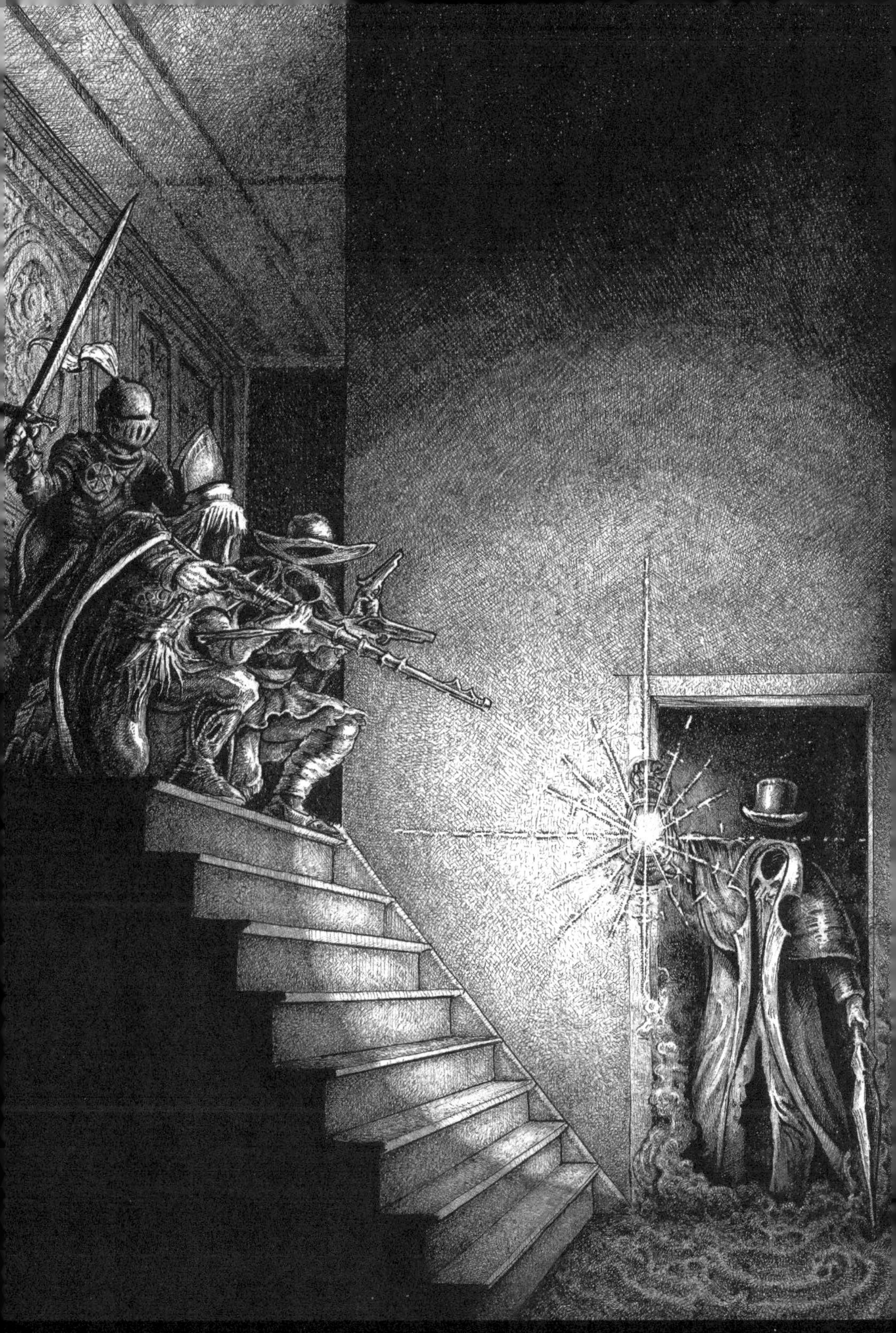

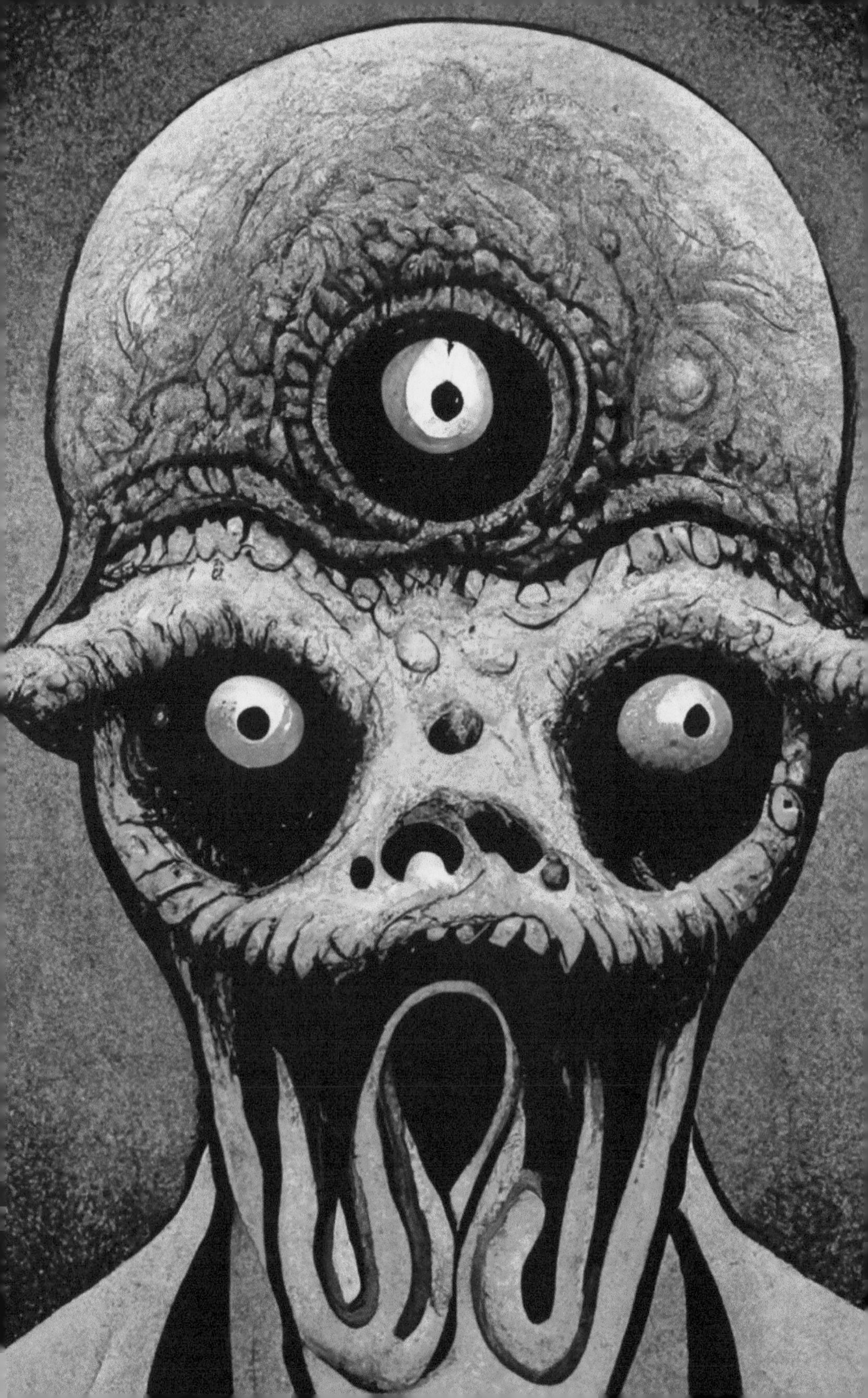

THE VAMPIRE ON THE TESSERACT WALL

by Larry Hodges

The realtor in red waved all twelve of her tentacles at the tesseract on the hill. "It's completely furnished and decorated, the perfect home for a new homeowner of higher sensibilities like yourself."

CorqCorq

CorqCorq surveyed the house with all twenty-four of his eyes. It was larger than he needed, sizable in all four dimensions—altitude, longitude, latitude, and spissitude. What would he do with all the space? He was unmarried, but that was something he hoped to change. And he could afford it, with his new job as an actuary.

"Let's take a look inside," the realtor said. "The previous owner was an art collector. As you'll see, he specialized in live 3Ds. Lots of them!"

CorqCorq

CorqCorq nodded, and so they rolled up the hill on their 4D hyperspheres. The yard was a bit unkempt with vegetation at an intolerable altitude and spissitude, but he could hire a neighborhood kid to mow it. The house itself seemed well-kept. They rolled inside.

The warm old-house smell hit him like a hurricanic caress of his probisci, that familiar

SmokeCedarMold
RustDustOzone
MildewPaintBlossom scent of a long-used home. The walls themselves
were a cheery black. But the realtor hadn't exaggerated about the 3D.

"Wow!" he said. He stared simultaneously at all twenty-four walls,
with a live 3D centered on each. He recognized most of the caged 3D
beings that decorated the walls. There were Sirians, Cygnies, Centauris,
Teegardens, Solarians, and many more. Like all 3D beings, they stared
off to the side into their own dimensions, showing their silhouettes
and guts for tasteful aficionados of higher dimensions like himself. The
purple Sirian was pacing its cage on four legs, roaring every few minutes
at some unknown something it imagined.

As he watched, a small, wiggling being was released from the food
dispenser and fell to the ground. The Sirian snatched it up in its huge
jaws, splashing purple blood on the cage's walls and floor as it cut the
poor creature in two.

CorqCorq
CorqCorq watched the two pieces go down its throat and into its
acidic stomach, the front piece still wriggling slightly for a moment
before going still. The long, legless, orange Cygnie in the adjacent 3D
stuck out its long green tongue between the bars of its cage into the
Sirian's and began lapping up the spilled blood.

At the back of the room was a combustor, its flames giving the room its
cozy warmth.

CorqCorq
CorqCorq could imagine himself lying in front of it, his head on a pillow
and his hyperspheres resting on a stool, relaxing and enjoying his nights
and weekends, his day job of calculating death forgotten.

Then he noticed the Solarian in the 3D over the combustor. The skinny
biped lay unmoving on the floor of the cage. At the top of the cage, the
opening to the food dispenser was jammed by a glob of shapeless, grayish
food material.

CorqCorq
CorqCorq rolled near and nudged the Solarian with a tentacle. Its insides were still, including its heart. He sighed; it was deactivated, apparently
starved to death by a defective feeder.

"The 3D store is just two blocks away," said the realtor, who was also
observing the dead Solarian. "Best selection in the region!"

CorqCorq
CorqCorq nodded. The 3D over the combustor was the most prominent spot in the tesseract; he'd want to choose something himself, something distinctive. He smiled, not sure when he'd decided to buy the house, but the decision had been made. All that was left was the dickering.

CorqCorq
The following week, CorqCorq rolled into the 3D store. He'd already bought the house and moved his things in. All that was missing was the perfect 3D for over the combustor. It was time to explore.

The store was huge, with rows and rows of 3Ds of every kind. There were Still-Ds of every imaginable type, ranging from abstract to real—livescapes, landscapes, seascapes, starscapes, abscapes, and so on. But while

CorqCorq
some liked Still-Ds, CorqCorq wanted something with action. There were lots of 3D vidscapes, both real and animated, and he browsed some of them. But soon, he was in the life-vid area. He roved up and down and sideways through the aisles, often stopping to look at the caged beings from planets all over the local region of a nearby 3D galaxy. Soon he was in the Solarian section.

He recognized some of the creatures from the exobiology classes he'd taken years ago in school, and from art museums. There were elephants and giraffes, sharks and whales, snakes and polar bears, squirrels and squids, and so much more. He spent hours examining each item. Several times he was on the verge of making a purchase, but each time he hesitated. They were close, but not quite what he was looking for. He wanted something just right, something perfect.

A salesman came over. There was something unhealthy about his pinkish rather than yellow skin, a sign of long-term dietary problems and lack of exercise, and half his eyes were clouded over.

CorqCorq
CorqCorq's actuarial mind slowly shook its head. "We have a special to-day, ten percent off everything!" said the salesman. "You can choose from our current stock or browse and choose directly from the Solarian planet itself. Have an idea of what you're look for?"

CorqCorq

"Just something really nice," CorqCorq said. "Something unique and interesting. But I haven't found it yet."

"Why not browse the planet itself? The viewer is preset for lots of interesting stuff. The dominant life is humans, so perhaps start with them?"

"Could you give me a tour of some of the best stuff?"

"Sure!"

A moment later, they were looking in on a man at a desk talking to others in a fancy looking oval room. There were 2D paintings on the wall, with the subjects looking out into the 3D world in the bizarre way that some 3D species liked to do with such artwork. It made no sense, since of course a 2D being couldn't look out into the 3D world any more than a 3D being could look out into a 4D world. A 2D being would have its eyes on its side so it could look out into its 2D world. Moving its eyes into its body would simply blind it from its own world. Some claimed that they were 2D representations of 3D beings, but that made no sense. Why not simply represent the 3D beings with 3D images? Statues!

"This human is the president of a large landmass called the United States," said the salesman. "He's considered the most powerful human on the whole planet. Imagine having him on your mantelpiece!"

CorqCorq

That would be incredible, thought CorqCorq. "How much is it?"

"It's our best item, the most exclusive, and the most unique piece we have," said the salesman. "Imagine inviting your friends over to see it!"

"Yes, but how much does it cost?"

MintEmerald

"Your friend will turn L i m e O l i v e with envy!" continued the salesman.

CorqCorq

"How much!" CorqCorq practically shouted.

"You can have it for the low, low price of one million shings. That's practically giving it away! It's one of a kind! You'll never regret it!"

CorqCorq

CorqCorq took a deep breath. He couldn't afford a million. There had to be something cheaper. Besides, he didn't like this human's weird-looking orange hair, like an explosion of 2D lines curving through space in impossible ways.

"Do you have something cheaper?"

Soon they were browsing through the planet. They observed humans labeled as "circus juggler," "banjo player," "Olympic ping-pong player," "sumo wrestler," and "mugger."

The last one seemed interesting. They watched as the tall human, dressed in dark clothing and cap, and holding a small projectile weapon in a pocket, stood near a dark alley late at night. Then a much shorter human walked by, glanced at the mugger, stopped, then walked into the alley. The mugger glanced in both directions, pulled the cap down over its face into some sort of mask, and then followed the short one into the shadowy alley. It raised its gun at the short one and held out a hand.

"A mugger is a criminal," explained the salesman. "It is demanding money from the shorter person, a female of the species. If the female does not give it money, the mugger will deactivate it with the weapon it holds and then take the money anyway."

"Why doesn't the mugger just deactivate the female and take the money?"

"I would guess it doesn't want to waste a bullet," said the salesman. "They cost money."

"Why isn't the female giving the mugger its money?" The two humans were staring at each other, both with eyes wide. Didn't humans blink to keep their eyes clean and wet? But those eyes…he stared at the female's and could barely look away. It was like looking into the heart of a black hole, pulling him closer, closer, as if its mass could affect something outside its flat 3D universe.

The woman was dressed even darker than the mugger, in pure black that went down to its black boots, which matched its long, black hair. In contrast, its skin was pale white. Then the female opened its mouth, exposing

CorqCorq

long, white, pointy teeth. That shook CorqCorq from his reverie.

"Something's wrong here," said the salesman. "Humans don't have teeth like that." They both leaned closer as they watched. The female pulled the mugger in close and sunk its teeth into its neck. The mugger jerked and then went still as bits of red blood dribbled down its neck. Its heart stopped beating.

A few minutes later, the female tossed the mugger's dead body aside. It pulled a white cloth from a pocket and wiped the blood from its mouth. Then it walked back to the entrance of the alley, glanced in both directions, and walked out. The viewer kept up with it as it walked away.

CorqCorq

"I want that one!" said CorqCorq.

"You sure?" asked the salesman. "It's not a normal human, it's—"

"That's the one I want." He wasn't sure why, he just knew.

The salesman shrugged his twelve shoulders. "The customer's always right. I'll bag it." He picked up a 3D steel cage nearby and pushed it through the viewer. The barred cage appeared around the female, caging it on all six sides simultaneously. It screamed and grabbed at the bars.

"We'll have it for you in a moment," said the salesman, reaching in with his tentacles to pull out the cage with the woman—but he stopped. The female was straining at the bars, and they began to bend. "She's a strong one!" he exclaimed. The female quickly squeezed out of the cage and tossed it aside like a toy.

"We'll use double-sized bars with carbon steel," said the salesman. He pushed the new cage through the viewer, again enclosing the creature. Again it grabbed the bars and, straining a bit more than before, again bent the bars and stepped out. It tossed the second cage away and looked about its 3D world as if trying to figure out where the cages were coming from.

"You asked for it," said the salesman, and put a third cage through the viewer, again enveloping the creature. The creature grabbed the bars, straining. Slowly, very slowly, they began to bend.

"That's not possible! That's *solid titanium*!" As the bars continued to bend, a wheeled vehicle with flashing lights approached. The female let go of the bars and shrank back, hiding its face with its hands.

CorqCorq

"I don't think it likes those lights," said CorqCorq. "Maybe give it more light?"

"Good idea," said the salesman. He held up a light stick and aimed light into the viewer. The female screamed and fell to the ground, curling into a ball.

"We'll have to use the neutronium cage," said the salesman. "But that's going to cost extra. A *lot* extra."

CorqCorq

"How much?" As CorqCorq spoke, the female stood up, its eyes tightly closed. After feeling about, it grabbed the bars of the cage and bent them enough to make its escape. "Okay, whatever the cost, use the neutronium!"

The female stepped out of the third cage and in a fury, slammed it against the nearby wall, shattering the building as the cage disappeared inside. The salesman practically threw the neutronium cage around the woman, the cage barely big enough to contain her small size.

The female kept its eyes closed as it screamed and grabbed at the neutronium bars. Its face reddened slightly as it strained. It grunted and then gave out such a shriek that nearby windows shattered, and the wall it had thrown the previous cage through tottered over and fell onto the cage, breaking apart in an explosion of bricks and mortar. It put its feet on the bars for leverage and pulled at the bars, its teeth showing as it strained. The sleeves covering its arms burst open, revealing bulging muscles that looked ready to pop.

But the bars held.

CorqCorq

CorqCorq lay in front of his combustor an hour later, head on a pillow and his hyperspheres resting on a stool, relaxing as he stared up at his prize with most of his eyes. The light was dim with the lights off and only a soft glow emanated from the combustor. The female stood in its cage, staring off into 3D space as he stared at its insides. Its body was no different than normal humans other than the pale skin and pointed teeth...and then he noticed its heart. It wasn't beating. Had it died already? But no, it occasionally moved about in its tight cage and kept looking side to side.

Its eyes, each a black dot surrounded by dark blue, surrounded by white, squinted as if the lighting from the combustor was too bright. What did the world look like to a 3D being? Probably pretty boring, he thought. But of course, 3D beings couldn't think, so that didn't matter. And yet, there was something behind those eyes, he was sure of it. Or at least sure of the illusion of it. He couldn't stop staring at them. One of them twitched, startling him as he jerked back involuntarily.

Several times, the magnificent creature grabbed the bars of its cage, trying again to bend and even to bite them, but the neutronium held. Then it went back to surveying its 3D environment through those squinting, sometimes twitching eyes.

A food dispenser at the top periodically dropped bits of common human food into the cage, but they lay untouched on the floor—a cheeseburger, fries, pepperoni pizza, Caesar salad, and bottle of Coke. Hopefully he'd find something that the creature could eat before it starved and deactivated.

He would never let that happen. He felt he could spend hours, days, an eternity just watching this creature. It didn't make sense, it was just one of many decorations on his walls, and yet...something was different. It was the eyes. Alien eyes, and yet so...un-alien. The creature had a tattoo of a bat on its neck, wore numerous necklaces, and had jeweled rings on every finger. Its nearly white face was thin, with papery skin, a tiny nose, and pale red lips. And yet, he only noticed these things in a rather perfunctory way as they were like a sun's corona to the sun itself, which was her eyes.

After many hours, and with great difficulty, he finally got up to go to bed, then stopped. Just for a moment, he'd sworn the creature had glanced out of its 3D world. But that was not possible. For it to do so, the eyes would have to point out of its 3D world, which required a dimension the creature did not have, spissitude. It was a 3D being and so could only look about its 3D world. And that's what it was back to doing. It had just been an illusion or an odd flicker of light. He needed to rest his eyes.

🦇

The following morning, he stared at the creature while he ate breakfast. He lost track of time and so was late to work—not a good thing for a new employee. He'd have to set an alarm next time he gazed at the creature.

As an actuary at a life insurance company, he spent his days over the surfaces of his desk inputting info to calculate the average life expectancy of his fellow beings. He had to be careful; if he was off by even a thousand years it would cost his company money, and of course those losses would be reflected in his paycheck. With the purchase of the expensive 3D, he couldn't afford to mess up. But he was good at his job and didn't make mistakes. They called him the Calculator—often he could just look people over from all four directions and unerringly calculate when they'd die. The realtor, for example, was rather healthy, probably had ten thousand years left. The 3D salesman with the yellow skin—not so healthy, probably a thousand years at most. He himself was in good health and knew he had many tens of thousands of years to go.

He returned home quickly after work, looking forward to an evening of relaxation. His new house was only a few blocks from work and so he now wheeled home, great exercise but leaving him a little tired. Soon he was back in front of the combustor, head on the pillow and wheels propped up on a stool.

There were tiny bite marks on one of the expensive neutronium bars. Had it really done that? Did it have any idea how much that cage had cost? But it was worth it. He stared at the non-beating heart inside its body. Someday he'd have to bring in an expert to explain that. Maybe humans can turn them on and off at will.

Once again, he stared at the creature as it looked about its 3D world with those squinting, mesmerizing dark eyes that slowly darted about, occasionally twitching. For a split second, they seemed to almost turn toward him, but that was, once again, just an illusion. Immediately afterward, the female grabbed at its head with both hands as if in pain. Then it continued to look about.

And then, slowly, very slowly, the face rotated in a way that didn't seem possible, going a bit fuzzy for a second. Its face contorted and went blurry again and then rotated some more. And then it rotated its head and stared directly out of the 3D and into the spissitude dimension of the 4D world.

CorqCorq

CorqCorq leaped to his wheels. "That's not possible!" he exclaimed as he watched the female slowly survey the tesseract room. Maybe an artist could create artwork that gave the illusion of that, like the 2D images on a 3D world that were so often depicted looking out of their 2D worlds, but not a real living being! It would be like a 2D being moving its eyes from its side, where it could look out into the 2D realm, and into its own body, blinding it to its 2D world while staring out into a dimension it wasn't designed to see and couldn't even perceive.

Then he realized that the creature was looking directly at him. It smiled.

He remembered the 3D facial expression from his exobiology studies in school. But why was the unthinking being grinning? More importantly, *how* was it looking at him?

"Hello," it suddenly said. "Could you dim the light?"

He lurched backwards, barely keeping on his wheels. Then he slowly returned, staring at the creature. It had to be some sort of art trick. A pre-recorded message? Or was it possible, just possible, that the creature itself had actually said that? Could a 3D being do that? No, it wasn't possible. And yet...

The female looked directly into his eyes, somehow staring at all twenty-four with her two, while he stared back with all twenty-four. There was something about that look, something that attracted and soothed and pulled at him. He wanted to look into them forever, forever, forever, and he leaned closer and closer and closer...

It had taken her a while to locate the source of the energy, but she'd found it, in a direction she didn't know existed. She was not of Earth, perhaps not of its universe, and didn't know her origin nor that of her fellow vampires. Maybe her ancestors had powers that had long gone dormant. But this new source of energy was far more powerful and satiating than anything she'd ever consumed—like eating meat after eons of grazing on grass. When the flickering creature had finally come into full view, she'd pulled it into her 3D world, but just a tiny bit, only the very top section of what apparently was its head. Then she'd bitten into it and found glory and power she had never tasted before!

She continued pulling it in, sucking each section dry before moving onto the next, until she was nearly saturated, and she'd barely begun her feast. With her handkerchief, she gently wiped the alien gore from her mouth. Now with ease, she pulled apart the neutronium bars of her cage and stepped out, like a flapping piece of plastic in a 3D world, everything increased by one dimension. She lowered the combustor to a minimum setting to cut the lighting to a more comfortable level. She surveyed the various exotic creatures on the walls and listened to their various hoots, hisses, and roars, and sniffed at the mostly distasteful smells. Perhaps before she would have found them interesting—and tasteful energy sources—but now they too were like grass to her. This weird new dimension had inspired a moment of wonder when she'd first saw it. But now, she realized, it was just one more dimension.

She returned to her tiny cage, stepped back in, and bent the bars back into place. She moved to the back and pulled on two of those bars, stretching them downward and inward until she had formed a neutronium chair. Then she sat down. She pulled in another segment and continued feasting, bit by bit, smiling in ecstasy. Would this heaven ever end?

Surely there would be more.

The realtor in red couldn't stop grinning. She'd sold the house just weeks ago, but the new owner, after paying full price, had disappeared. And so, she got to sell it again. Double commission! She was currently showing it to another prospective owner, a family of four who'd already expressed interest in the 3Ds, and it was selling time!

She began her usual spiel, waving all twelve of her tentacles at the tesseract on the hill. "It's completely furnished and decorated, the perfect home for a new homeowner of higher sensibilities like yourself."

NIGHT SHIFT

A WORLD CAUGHT BETWEEN
LOST ARCANE HISTORY AND
ENGINEERED EVOLUTION

UNRAVEL THE SECRETS
OF ECHOR CITY AND THE
AUGUR CORPORATION

NIGHT SHIFT: AN URBAN FANTASY AUDIO DRAMA

SEASON ONE AVAILABLE NOW ON ALL
PODCAST PLATFORMS

WWW.NIGHTSHIFTPOD.COM

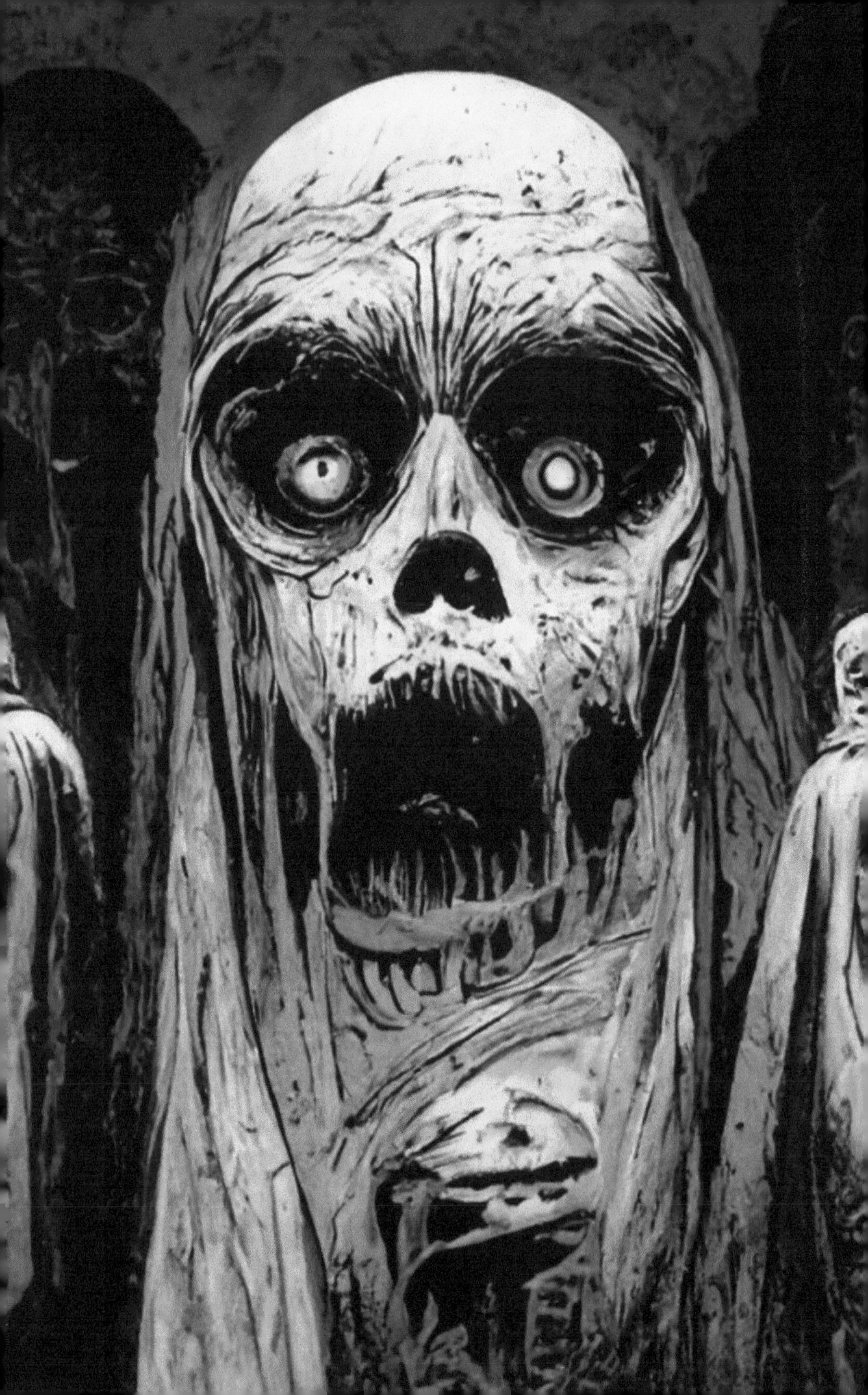

IMMATERIAL WITNESS

by Graham J. Darling

They don't mean to frighten, but they want something so much, it's unsettling. They want it enough to come back from the dead—or to never quite die, we don't know which. Like the so-called "dark matter" that astronomers talk about, or like living souls for all that, we can see what they do but only guess what they are.

It's justice they want. From the man in chains who led the Stoic to a secret grave, as Pliny tells; through the stern dead King of Denmark, the pitiful phantom of Greenbrier County, the terrible *onryō* of Japan, down to the present day—ghosts want justice. And I tell them what I tell everyone: "Hear ye, hear ye, this court is now in session. Let all who have dealings or interests draw nigh and give their attention. God save this honorable court!"

As singular a case as this proved to be, it opened routinely enough. In a bright oak-paneled courtroom, with me below the bench to manage the flow of persons and the capture of their every word, soon the brushstrokes of traditional witness testimony painted a clear picture of these uncontested facts: Simon Vaughan, accountant, divorced, having suffered a stroke that left him blind and bedridden, asked to be prescribed a lethal drug, as is legal in this state. His long-time doctor refused, as is also broadly legal (though subject to discipline by the Medical

Board), and instead offered to help him cope with his new condition. Following this conversation, Simon shopped around till he got what he wanted from a specialist (that is, one whose practice comprises nothing else): a small bottle containing a single "goodbye pill" that was a layered mix of antiemetic, sedative, and time-release cardiotoxin.

He called a family meeting to take his leave: his children, Michael and Joanne, both in their twenties and settled in other parts of town; his brother, Harold, flown in from the coast. Though once all had assembled in the split-level manse that had raised crop after crop of Vaughans, Simon surprised everyone, including apparently himself, by also asking for a priest—"to tie up the loose ends," he said.

Father Greene soon arrived, soaked from the rain, and met with him privately for over an hour. Then the family was called back into the lily-choked master bedroom, where the good Father read out a letter he said Simon had dictated, renouncing the proposed suicide and requesting their support in getting a disabled man through a difficult time. When the brother then asked if this was really what he wanted, Simon Vaughan replied, "I want to hold my grandchild."

Greene asked for the poison, but it had gone missing, and a search of the house failed to find it. Once he'd left, and while Simon rested, the able-bodied Vaughans took council in their old living room. Joanne first raged against meddling clerics, then complained she'd already kicked out the loser who'd been living with her and was only postponing the abortion to spare Dad's feelings, and was she now to quit her studies and put her life on hold? Michael ventured that maybe he and she could move back home to look after their father, at least until they could get him into long-term care; it wouldn't be forever. Eventually, Joanne agreed—she'd come to feel the pinch, paying for her whole apartment herself. Uncle Harold regretted he must return to his own family on the coast.

They returned upstairs for another conference with the invalid, which ended with Joanne saying, "We will always respect your choice, Dad, whatever it is, whenever it is," as she replaced the pill bottle on the nightstand beside him with an audible click.

Two weeks passed, and the three settled into routine. Simon Vaughan listened to audiobooks and began to learn braille. Joanne stayed in the house with him during the day, then left for evening class when Michael came home from work. After finishing his own dinner that Joanne had left him, Michael would bring Simon's portion upstairs to wake him from his afternoon nap and help him eat.

It was Michael Vaughan's sworn and trembling account that, after he knocked and entered the bedroom that sad day, he found his father dead, holding the open and empty bottle in folded hands. But his suspicions were roused, he said, by the state of the bedclothes, which seemed too tucked in for that hour, and by other signs that the body had been arranged after death. Plus, he had not thought the afflicted man could remove the childproof cap with his shaking hands, though admitted on cross-examination that, given enough time and determination, it might've been possible. Anyway, instead of the funeral home, he phoned the police, who eventually charged Joanne Vaughan with murder.

The coroner testified. The police detective testified. The terms of the will and other documents were entered into the record. The jury was briefed on what next to expect.

Then the proceedings were adjourned elsewhere. In part, that is, since the new venue, even stripped of superfluous furniture, could not have held Judge Vargas and the twelve jurors, much less the many spectators attending this sensational trial. These all remained at the courthouse, sitting in their usual places but watching the monitors set up at the empty prosecution and defense tables and on the witness stand. Those displays were fed live from cameras trained on us, the key players in this timeless drama: Chung, the prosecutor, an earnest young woman; the serene and affable McKenny for the defense; the glowering Joanne Vaughan, of course, for everyone has the right to face their accuser; Michael Vaughan, as legal guardian for an effectively incapacitated person; and I, secure in my robes and office of Clerk of the Court and surrounded by my equipment, ready to transmit what transpired here, and to call the State's final witness in the only place possible—back in the bedroom of the Vaughan family home, scene of the alleged crime.

Early researchers had shown that those feelings traditionally associated with ghosts could all be explained by natural phenomena: the sense of awe and dread, from the infrasound of wind blowing through cloisters or down chimneys to set one's insides quivering in resonance, while the equally cliché cold spots and clamminess were also far more typical of houses once-upon-a-time than today.

Then later researchers showed that, when these same conditions of low temperature, high humidity, and pulsing pressure were deliberately applied in certain locales, ghosts, in fact, appeared.

It turns out that this combination produces a supersaturated atmosphere like the inside of a Wilson cloud chamber, the device that won the Nobel Prize in Physics for both 1927 and 1948 and, ironically, that was originally invented to recreate eerie occurrences, like the so-called "Brocken specter" that alpinists talk about. In that pregnant environment, a single passing subatomic particle leaves a visible vapor trail, and, evidently, other subtle influences can also stand revealed.

Preliminary tests (kits are now available in every drugstore) had shown the presence here of a potential manifestation. Now, over the stripped deathbed, I set up a clear plastic tent sealed to the floor with sand-socks, with five folding chairs around it, and all the room's windows covered with blackout cloth.

We took our seats, and at a signal from the prosecutor, I then dimmed the overhead lights, switched on the subwoofer and hooded lamps, alternated between admitting steam and chilled nitrogen with the precision of an anesthesiologist, and intoned: "Simon Vaughan, come forth!"

Soon congealed the form of a balding man that matched the photo I held. Its eyes were closed and its chest rose and fell in sleep as it lay translucent and aglow amidst the gentle sparkle of cosmic rays. My hair still rises at such times, and not solely from the sonics.

"Michael Vaughan!" Chung called out. The young man jumped and jerked his blanched face towards her. "Remembering that you are still under oath, do you vouch that this is Simon Vaughan, your father?"

Through chattering teeth, he replied, "...yes, yes I do. Dad, I..."

"Counsel for the defense," spoke the enlarged TV face that overhung the scene, "does your client wish to dispute the identity of this witness?"

"No, your Honor," said McKenny, briefly standing. Then everyone looked at me, sitting within arm's reach of the thing on the bed.

I leaned forward and quickly chanted: "Simon Arthur Vaughan, do you solemnly swear to present the truth, the whole truth, and nothing but the truth, so help you God?"

In an instant, the vaporous eyes were open and bulging—not as a man might blink them open, but like a jump cut in an avant-garde movie. The hands that had been peacefully lying at his side were suddenly fumbling around his chest, and the thin, white lips were moving. "...God..." echoed a tremulous voice from my photophone.

The next moment, all was as before.

I sat back again, straight-faced as ever, but inwardly pleased to find myself working with such a responsive witness. Often their impairment has left them with very limited vocabularies, and always with one-track minds. But when they do answer questions or react to their surroundings, it can be with a subtle intelligence and creativity that still marks them as human, rather than some kind of ethereal video recording. Sometimes our standard opening formula makes them vanish for good, but to leave it out, in our experience, tends to retain a class of witness that seems more interested in producing chaos and pain than accurate testimony. Though for the most part, by many signs and corroborations, ghosts have shown they want to tell the truth—are desperate to do so. Especially when approached in person.

Chung stepped up to the bedside. "Mister Vaughan," she said, "tell us, in your own way, what befell you here on the twelfth of last month."

For a minute more, the ghost of Simon Vaughan just lay and snored. Then indentations abruptly appeared on either side of his bristly chin, as if an unseen hand had grabbed him there, squeezing the lower lip, forcing open the mouth. "Ah, ah," said Simon Vaughan as he fought awake, then pulled free and turned away just as something pressed into his cheek. "What? Help!" he managed, before his head was again wrenched forward and jaw jerked down. He coughed and choked, then his hands came up and seemed to clutch at some rod-like object, but only as it was already being pulled away from his face (a six-inch "pill gun," once used to treat the ailing family dog, had earlier been produced with fresh human bite marks on its plastic shaft). Then he was left to lie, spent and shaking, blind eyes casting wildly about.

"God," he moaned, then "no, no." He felt at his neck, then further up and into his mouth, thrust two fingers down his throat and began to gag again. Then his hand was snatched away and forced to his side. A moment later, the other hand made its quivering way up his body and into his face before it too was seized and brought down.

This happened again and again, first on the one side, then the other. "Please," said Vaughan. "Please. Please."

Into the hushed and shrouded room burst an electronic jingle, the skeleton of a popular tune, repeated. "Bip bidibee-boop beeep. Bip bidibee-boop beeep."

Everyone started and looked around, except Joanne Vaughan. She cursed, tore open her purse and yanked out a smartphone. Then she stopped and stared at it in horror, then slowly turned towards the bed again, as did we all. The sound was coming from Simon Vaughan.

"Please, Jojo, please." The ringing ceased; the uneven combat, which had paused a moment, now resumed. Slower and slower moved Simon Vaughan, weaker and weaker. Then his hands could only twitch, plucking at the sheets. His eyes closed, his breathing deepened again. A few minutes later, it stopped; his body convulsed briefly, then was still.

Invisible fingers straightened his disheveled comb over, rearranged his hands and the phantom blankets, wiped the tears from his cheeks, then left him alone. Time passed, nothing changed. Then suddenly the tenuous body had shifted position and was breathing again.

Counselor McKenny and Joanne Vaughan conferred in the far corner of the bedroom. Beside me, Michael Vaughan heaved a shaking sigh.

Chung let the basic sequence run through once more to the end. Then she spoke again.

"Simon Vaughan, who was that with you when you died?"

Again, Vaughan was awake and fighting for his life. "Jojo, please," we heard. Then again, he was asleep.

Now leaning right over his plastic sarcophagus, she said very slowly and loudly: "Simon Vaughan, did you want to die?"

"No, no," said Simon Vaughan.

"Your Honor, the State rests its case." Chung returned to her chair at the foot of the bed. The ghost of Simon Vaughan began to fade and dissipate.

"Liar!" I screamed into its ear. "You're a lying liar, and we're going to prove it now!" The body on the bed snapped back into focus and flashed through a series of postures and sounds expressive of frustration, even rage.

We necromancers (the term is unsavory, but technically correct) have a long reputation of cruelty to the un-living, ever since Erichtho of Thessaly was whipping their corpses with bundles of live vipers. But, as Judge Vargas had also told the jury, what I did here to Simon Vaughan was in his best interest—it was in the interest of justice, which, as Plato explains, is in everyone's best interests, right down to the executed felon's. And right now, I could not let this ghost think its task on Earth was over before the cross-examination.

"Mister Vaughan," said McKenny, sliding forward. "This document was entered as Exhibit D. It states that you consent to assistance with your death by anyone at all, absolving all such persons from any criminal and civil liability, *especially* the manufacturers of 'Oblivin,' together with its prescribers, dispensers, and administers, now and forever. Do you deny you signed this?"

"…no…"

"Your Honor, the Defense moves for an immediate dismissal of all charges, with prejudice. No crime has been committed here, by the precedents of…"

"Objection, your Honor!"

"Counsel will approach the bench," said Judge Vargas. Chung and McKenny walked over to the judge's monitor high up in its own corner, and all three donned headsets and whispered together. Fingers tapped keypads as files flew invisibly back and forth. Joanne Vaughan smirked; Michael Vaughan stared at the floor. Simon Vaughan seemed stabilized; I tended to my switches and valves.

After a few minutes, the attorneys resumed their seats and the judge spoke off screen. "Members of the jury, I have taken the matter under submission. My final ruling on it, along with other points of law relating to this case, will be part of my instruction before you retire to consider your verdict. But for now, you are to focus on points of fact and continue to hear evidence while this witness is available." Then, back to us, he said, "Counsel for the Defense, proceed."

McKenny shrugged, smiled, and turned again to the bed. "Mister Vaughan, at the time of your death, as we have heard, you were quite blind. How exactly do you know it was Joanne Vaughan who was with you when you died?"

"Bip bidibee-boop beeep," went Simon Vaughan.

"The distinctive ring of her mobile phone?"

"Bip bidibee-boop beeep."

"Which you would recognize anywhere?"

"Bip bidibee-boop beeep."

"Did it sound like…this?" McKenny held up a phablet, pressed its screen. "Bip bidibee-boop beeep."

"Jojo," said Simon Vaughan.

"Wrong, Mister Vaughan! In fact, this is my own device, which moments ago I easily reprogrammed to emit exactly that ringtone. Mister Vaughan," McKenny almost whispered now, "think. What other way could you have known it was Joanne who was with you?"

Silence. McKenny let it stretch a full minute.

"Mister Vaughan," he said. "Have you any other reason to believe it was her and not…someone else?"

"…no…"

"Someone else with a portable phone." He looked around the room—we all had one showing. "Someone else who knew Joanne and her ringtone, and from that, hatched a plan to deceive you then, and mislead us now. Someone else who would be in the house alone with you around that time. Someone else who, by your last will, stood to inherit almost nothing after Joanne and her child, but everything should her claim be nullified by a conviction of murder. Someone else like—" He whirled and pointed, "—her brother, Michael Vaughan!"

Michael Vaughan shot to his feet, swayed, and collapsed in a faint.

In vain would Chung, in her closing argument, cite *L'affaire des poisons*, the epidemic of "inheritance powders" that decimated seventeenth-century France, reaching into the highest of circles and only halted by the sternest of measures. In vain would she suggest a conspiracy of the siblings to further seize and split the substantial insurance that would've been voided by a suicide, but not by a murder, even one by "parties unknown." McKenny had established reasonable doubt, and where there is reasonable doubt, there can be no conviction. Both Vaughan heirs would go free, though murder lived among them.

"The witness is dismissed," said the judge, but Simon Vaughan did not fade, and showed no sign that he ever would. "…no…please…God…help…help…no…" He just kept shuffling through his last moments until my own last moment when I had to turn off my machinery and fold my tent. But I knew he was still there, writhing, and always would be, though his bed be burned and his home demolished so that never again could he materialize to remind us of our shame (as with that bathhouse in Ancient Greece, that palace chamber in Han China, that rectory in Regency England).

Him and so many others like him—in bad hours I picture them everywhere—heaped on my desk, crowded around my chair, in the air, underfoot, writhing, pleading, writhing…

Ghosts want justice. We all want justice.

We don't always get it.

Episode 1

www.rpgforyouandme.com

RPG for You and Me is a sci-fantasy podcast in an original world! Our main show Neon Heat happily straddles the line of actual play vs audio drama with professional production, a synthwave soundtrack, tightly edited for your enjoyment. A love letter to Mass Effect, Persona, X-Men, Dresden Files, and more that adds up to heaps of anime drama, with a dash of romance. Please join our heroine Athena and her friends as they navigate a wide sweeping conspiracy in a post-cataclysm world, rebounding full of hope rather than despair.

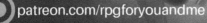 patreon.com/rpgforyouandme   @rpgforyouandme

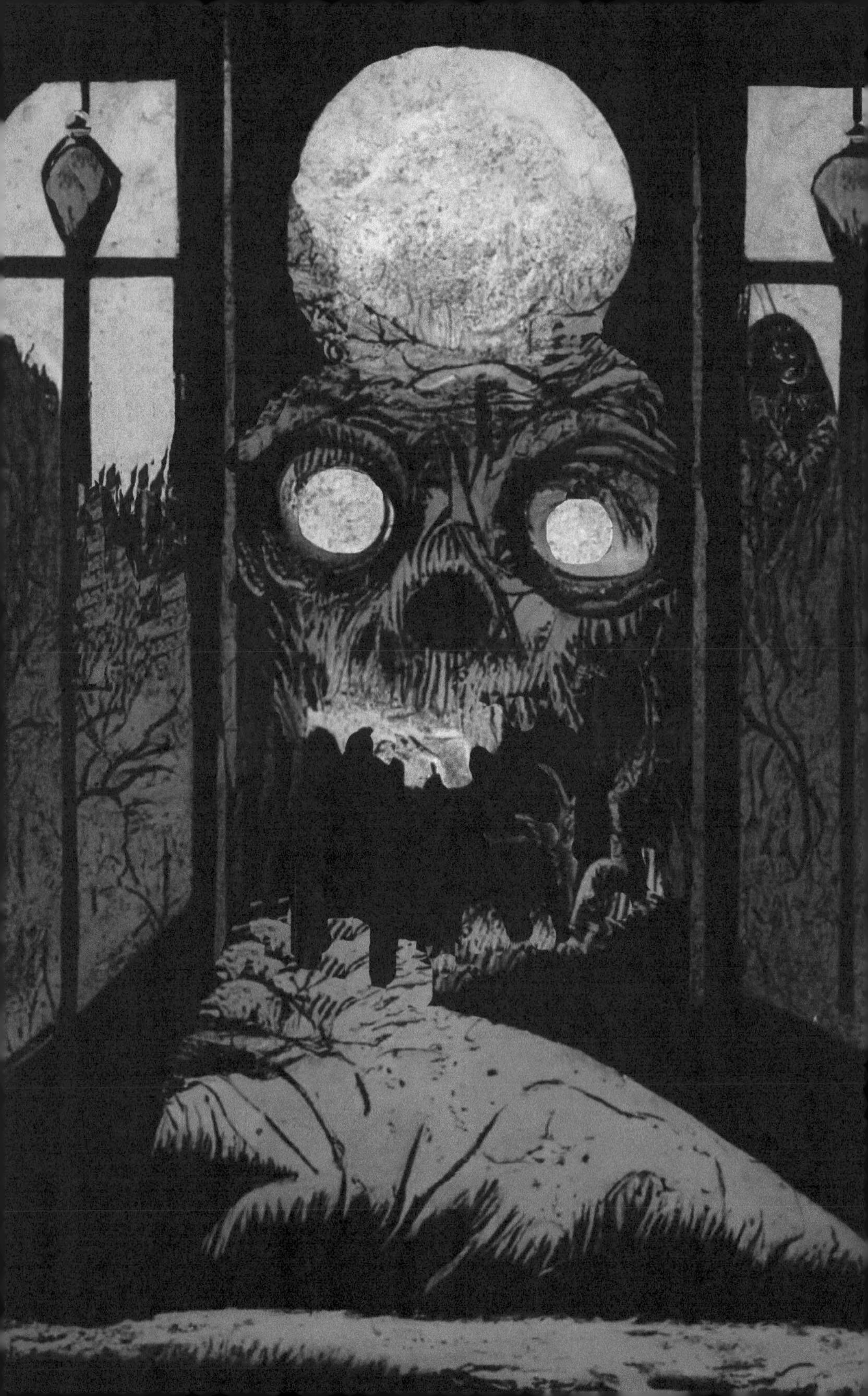

A PIECE MISSING

by S. J. Townend

A ll six screaming monitors, gathered like nestling owlets in the pocket of her apron, fall silent as soon as she crosses the threshold. The distress of the baby had been hideous to hear, but the silence which follows—as the monitors return to a lowly crackle of static interference—feels asphyxiating. Back inside, she can no longer hear the baby. Her baby. Had it been her baby she had heard?

Up the stairs her feet carry her, as they have a thousand times before, along the hallway towards the furthest room, which is also the smallest. The door, like her front door, like all doors in her home, which has become her house—a house—is stoppered open, wedged fully ajar, and the winds pushing in through the open windows make ghosts of the delicate white curtains.

The cot bed lies empty like the rest of the hollow room. A monitor crackles gently with static atop the small mattress.

She draws her arms tight around herself and rubs the sides of her bare arms muddy palms that are red and raw beneath. She doesn't notice how filthy her hands are though. Her mind is on other things, in other places. She can't see the dirt, or perhaps, she chooses not to.

Despite her chill, she can't pull down the window. *What if what I've lost wants to return?* she thinks.

Not here. Whatever I am looking for is not here. Perhaps the next room?

She moves through every room, checks in all the cupboards, searches and pries under stale bedding, under each dusty cushion. Nada. The breeze continues to move in and out of the building, like air through lungs, and gives a dusting of goosebumps to her skin. She finds nothing. Zilch.

The staircase groans as she makes her way down to search the ground floor. It is as if the house feels her despair. *Why am I so sad? Is this not what I wanted?* She continues on her search and makes her way through to the last room which she has not yet checked: the kitchen. She sees within a moment that what she's searching for is not here. In her heart, she knows she'll not find it here or maybe anywhere, especially not in the kitchen where cutlery and unsafe things are kept. What she does find, though, is a mountain of dirty dishes. All of her dishes have been used. They clutter the countertop. The washing up seems endless in her home. Her house. A house.

She slides her finger over the smooth curve of a greasy plate and, on noticing the brown crescent of dirt beneath each of her fingernails, she lifts the plate up and decides now would be a good a time as any to wash it. *My hands will benefit from the chore.* On touching the plate, she forgets what she's been searching for, forgets why she's in the kitchen, has a feeling like the feeling one gets when one moves from one room to another in search of something, forgetting what it is they're searching for the moment they cross over.

She fills up the sink with warm, soapy suds. Dipping her sullied hands into it, pushing them deep below the surface until they can't be seen any more, will provide some release, she hopes.

No time like the present. She sighs. She is not sure what time it is because the wall-mounted clock has been stuck for a long time. Its second-hand clicks on beat like a metronome but never advances past twelve. It has been five till three for days now. Perhaps a month. *Does it need a new battery? Or maybe it's beyond repair.* "Sometimes, things do break beyond repair." She says this aloud and hears herself saying it, but it does not sound like her voice. Is it a recording of her voice? *Was that a recording of my voice?* she thinks. She says the words aloud again to be sure. But she can't be sure of anything.

I might be stuck here at the sink forever if the clock cannot be fixed. The pile of dirty plates looms—seems to lengthen like shadows at dusk. She makes a start on it, and many ticks of the clock pass by as she soaks and scrubs and rinses the mound of dirty porcelain, but the stack never seems to deplete.

She rubs her tired eyes with the part of her arm just between the elbow and her wrist, which she cannot for the life of her name. Upon opening her eyes, she finds she is no longer at the helm of her own kitchen, taking pride in its appearance, its order, but is standing at a sink she does not recognize, washing dishes she has no memory of using.

The big hand of the clock is still stuck between two and three, and the little hand on the eleven. The tile pattern of the kitchen's backsplash seems familiar. *This must be home*, she thinks, the constants in the house giving her some reassurance.

She sees a translucent version of herself in the sheen of the glass in the window above the kitchen sink, and she thinks she sees a streak of bloodied dirt on her left cheek, or maybe on her right—she has never been very good at understanding reflections—so she soaks and wrings a clean cloth, which she always keeps tucked behind the faucet.

The windowsill, she thinks as she tries to recall how the mark may have been made, *is made of the most beautiful tapestry of glazed tiles*. She dabs at the mark on her cheek again and again; and rubs until it fades. She then returns her focus to the dishes.

The largest plate is precariously balanced atop the dirty dish pile. She carefully pulls it free and places it into the water and finds a rhythm with the *tick, tick* passing of stationary time. She still is making no progress, as the pile of dirty dishes continues to increase, but at least, she notices, her hands are becoming cleaner, free of grime. The baby monitors in her apron still just crackle quietly, yielding no clues.

She lifts an oval serving dish, which perhaps a roast turkey had been presented on, carved up into smaller morsels, served as brown slices onto myriad of smaller dining plates. All from a meal perhaps reminiscent of happier times. Still, it is a meal she does not remember cooking, or eating. She submerges the plate in water. She scrubs off the grease and minuscule fibers of meat, buffs the center of the dish, then she screams *Fuck!* and drops the dish down into the water again.

She gingerly lifts the plate back out and brings it closer to her tired eyes for examination.

There, within the markings of the fat from the cooked bird's carcass, she sees an imprint of a familiar face. Drawing a deep breath, she feels a rush of something not altogether awful nor altogether pleasant quicksilver through her veins. *It's him*, she thinks. *Husband.* She traces over the sticky brown lines, which swerve and bend and twist and straighten and portray the face of her husband. It's not his sleeping face, his face full of laughter or sadness, his cross face he makes when he reprimands her for leaving the front door wide open. It's the face only she will recognize (or so she hopes): his face at orgasm.

This is the last face of his she remembers. It is the last clear memory she has of her husband. They haven't made love in over a year. She tries to remember if she has seen him since then, since he last came inside of her. She presses the base of her palm against her forehead in thought. He is still living in the house. This she knows because she's seen his large shoes resting by the front door. Also, she can the shed out back through the kitchen window, and the door is open to the garden. She looks through her own faint reflection, out towards the acre of land on which the house sits. *His shed. That is where he often is,* she recalls, *pottering, or doing something with French beans. And if he is not here, living with her, then the shed door would not be open. My husband is quite green-fingered; a keen gardener. But when did I last study his face?*

In the image of him on the cream plate in her hands, she sees his eyes are closed. His head is tipped back, but his mouth is wide open, chin nearly touching his chest. Wide open like every door and window in the house.

She rubs her eyes, and in the pop of a bubble, the image is gone. Such a strange sight to behold. Had she imagined it? She moves on to the next dirty plate. *What a strange day,* she thinks. *What an odd vision.*

She works her way through a few more plates, trance-like, finding the repetition of the chore meditative. She looks down at another plate, and this time, does not feel as surprised to see another image. This time, it is less clear, but it is there: coiled spine, disproportionately large eyes, small nubs. She sees it clearly, and when she scrubs harder, the image appears stronger. It is an embryo…no, a fetus.

She places the plate down in the suds and pulls it from the water again. This time, the fetus is swollen. It appears larger, more refined, as if a trimester has passed: clear limbs, a defined nose, an umbilical cord. Before, she'd seen only smears of gravy. She dips and lifts the plate again, scrubs the image with the sponge, each wipe in time with the click of the stuck clock. The image mutates. It twists and spins until the fetus has the face of a child. A baby. Her baby?

Its eyes are like her husband's had been in the image of him: screwed closed. People used to tell her they could see his face in it, the baby.

She has a clear memory—perhaps the only crisp memory she'll have this day—of the baby. She remembers the shade of red its cheeks turned, and the noise it made when nothing she could do would settle it. Could it, could this, be her baby, this face on a fetus on a dirty dinner plate?

Her heart is confused. It is trying to beat in time with the stuck clock hand, but the rhythm is syncopated, faster, lost. Her heartbeat and the clock are the only sounds she can hear. The baby monitors are silent.

She hesitates before dipping the plate again. She's fearful the baby's face may vanish, but she's also keen to end this delusion. She dips the plate, then pulls it up and out of the suds again. The face is gone, but a new image has appeared. She turns the plate like the steering wheel of a car, until she finds its correct position, until she can see what the plate wants to show her.

It's a tree this time. Not a face, a willow tree. Drooping branches hang heavy to the right, while the trunk bows slightly to the left. *I know this tree*, she thinks. She recognizes this tree because it is the tree at the far end of the garden.

She drops the plate into the sink. Foam explodes onto the countertops. She reaches into her apron pocket and holds the monitors tight so that they cannot escape. She runs out of the house and into the backyard. She keeps on running past the shed, its door still ajar.

She hops and leaps and bounds over scattered terracotta pots, and spades, and bundles of bamboo cane, and sacks of fertilizer.

"Love, what's up?" she hears. The words are spoken by a tall, gaunt shadow. It is a shadow which has thrown itself onto the garden. She knows this shape which is speaking, asking her if she is okay, calling her love, but she cannot see who, precisely, it is.

"I can't stop," she replies.

Where its face should be, she sees the face she saw on the plate. Not the sex face, but the face of a screaming child, a crying baby. Red cheeks, flaring tonsils, crying eyes which won't stop watering.

She hears again: "Love, what's up?" But she still sees the face of the baby.

She ignores the shadow with the gardening fork in its hand and picks up the pace. She must get to the tree. It is as if the plate has spoken to her, offered guidance in all the ways the expensive baby monitors she'd ordered—six-fold, one for each room—had failed.

The tree.

The willow tree which bows to the side. Maybe beneath the tree, she'll find what she thinks she's been searching for, been keeping the windows open for. What she has lost. Upon reaching the willow, she drops to her knees and places her hands on the mound of earth piled up high underneath it. *Feels cold to the touch. But there's nothing here. Just dirt, a tree.*

It is a tree which has been here for longer than she has—much longer— and she feels like she has been here already for an immeasurable length of time. A tear rolls down her cheek, weaves a wonky path. It meanders towards her chin, itself unsure if it is being shed in relief or in sadness. The tear rolls off face and drops to the mound of soil. In this moment, she has the urge to draw her own face closer to the heap. It is as if it is calling to her, this pile of earth which is stacked up under the willow tree.

Her lips are now kiss-close to the tip of the heap. *Should I?* she thinks, but she is doing what she is thinking of doing before she has had a chance to reason. Her tongue is probing into the mound, pressing against and into the mud, and her hands are scooping up more in preparation for her mouth.

The hunger overriding her is unquenchable. She tries to satiate it with what is in front of her by filling her mouth with several scoopfuls of mud. She chews on small clumps of soil and handfuls of grassy turf. She masticates until something hard hits her molars, something familiar. Something which is not food, not nutritious, not what she thinks she is looking for. It cracks hard against grinding teeth. She plays with it with her tongue, cleans it, and then with thumb and finger, pulls it out: a small, flat, piece of porcelain.

She admires the smooth, found treasure in her muddied palm. This is not like any of the porcelain she has ever served in her home, her house, a house; it is like no dish or plate she has ever washed or stacked. This piece is white with bold, blue shining lines, and navy hatched pictures. On this small piece, which is no larger than a coin, she sees the edge of a blue willow tree.

She strokes the painted blue branches with her fingertips. She admires the illustrated branches, similar to the ones that shelter her now. She sits on folded knees and continues to search the dirt for more broken pieces of chinoiserie-patterned pottery. With her tongue, she cleans each new piece she retrieves from the pile, greets each like a long-lost friend with her lips, and then arranges them on a patch of flattened grass beside her.

Without the constant click of the kitchen clock, she loses all awareness of time. She nearly loses herself completely in what she's doing, even though she isn't entirely sure why she's doing it. Her hands dig and scoop deeper. She pulls out piece after piece and with her tongue and saliva, cleans each of the organic matter and humus and grub larvae and other things which dwell in the dirt.

The shape of an old plate forms, and on it, she sees the story appear. This time, it is not a mirage, not her imagination, not anything she is unsure of, because this time, she knows the story to be real.

As a child, her own mother would tell the tale of the blue willow plate. She recalls her mother telling her the story while serving her sliced apples. Childhood memories etched into the stone of her mind. *To be the child and not the mother makes for happier times.*

In the collection of fragments, she sees the two lovers. One of the lovers, the woman, is promised to another man whom she does not love. She elopes with the man she does love, but they are caught and banished to a faraway island. The Gods take pity on them and transform the lovers into a pair of swallows who fly free.

The plate now lies in pieces on the grass, and is nearly complete, all apart from one missing piece. She knows the missing piece depicts the image of the two swallows who face each other in a permanent state of amorous conjunction. The sight of the incomplete plate deeply disturbs her, so she digs. She digs deeper and deeper, and searches for this last piece. But she knows deep within herself that she will never find it. The plate will remain fragmented, like her thoughts.

She spits soil, pebbles, and crushed snail shells from her mouth. She scoops with her hands until she strikes something hard and large with her fingertips. Clearing the layers of loosened dirt, she pulls up not one, but two items, each of a similar size. Her tears are coming hard and fast now, and each time she wipes her cheeks, more mud and dirt and blood from all the small cuts and scrapes on her hands, smear onto her face. She lays the two objects, body-like objects, side-by-side. She knows she has seen this before, this pair, but not in a dirty plate, nor in the blue willow story, nor in a dream. Perhaps in a dream, if *this* is a dream and not reality.

On the left lies a clumsily stuffed corpse, once a living baby. She probes the human sack and feels both sharp and smooth edges inside it. She remembers. *Yes! I emptied it of its pain, filled it with fragments of broken china.* To the right, almost identical, the mirror image—although she has never been very good at understanding reflection—is an old porcelain doll caked in the mud in which it was buried. She turns the doll over. Her finger traces where it's been broken and taped back up. *This one I filled with something crimson and wet, a material altogether softer. It holds the pain of the other within it. Afterwards, they both slept so well.*

It is then she becomes more disturbed and jumps up suddenly, because all six baby monitors start to scream at once. The burst of cries causes her to jump and fall backwards.

She s grabs the two lifeless bodies and places them back inside the hole, their hole. She rushes to fill the void with the piles of mud and grit and blue-white China pieces she recently dug up. The constant wailing from the baby monitors grows louder. She kicks the rest of the soil to finish covering the hole and runs back up to the garden. Her baby is back. She can hear it screaming. Somewhere, everywhere in the house, something is screaming. Her baby must've found its way back in. Somehow. She can hear her baby on the six monitors that are nestled in her apron pocket. Her baby. A baby. Did she have a baby?

With each step forward, her hold on the truth slips. As she nears her home, the house, a house, she sees the tall shadow leaning against the open shed. It talks to her, susurrates something, but all she hears is the persistent, piercing scream of a child calling her.

She looks to the tall shape's face. *Perhaps I can try to read its lips. It is speaking to me, trying to say something important, a clue.* But where nose, eyes, lips should be, she sees instead the face of a porcelain doll with willow buds bursting out through every one of its orifices. White-green, cotton-soft buds push through china nostrils, poke out like caged flora through ear holes and rosebud lips. The tall shape is not who she thought it would be. But who did she think it was? Her memory draws a blank. There are no hints or images or shadows in the space of her mind. She runs faster towards the house, dashes through the wide-open front door.

All six screaming monitors, gathered like nestling owlets in the pocket of her apron, fall silent as soon as she crosses the threshold. The distress of the baby had been hideous to hear, but the silence which follows—as the monitors return to a lowly crackle of static interference—feels asphyxiating. Back inside, she can no longer hear the baby. Her baby. Had it been her baby she had heard?

Up the stairs her feet carry her, as they have a thousand times before, along the hallway towards the furthest room which is also the smallest. The door, like her front door, like all doors in her home, which has become her house—a house—is stoppered open, wedged fully ajar, and the winds pushing in through the open windows make ghosts of the delicate white curtains.

Dark Matter Magazine
Issue Series
Collectible Soft Enamel Pins

Every issue of Dark Matter Magazine is commemorated with a limited edition soft enamel pin.

Never trust the living.

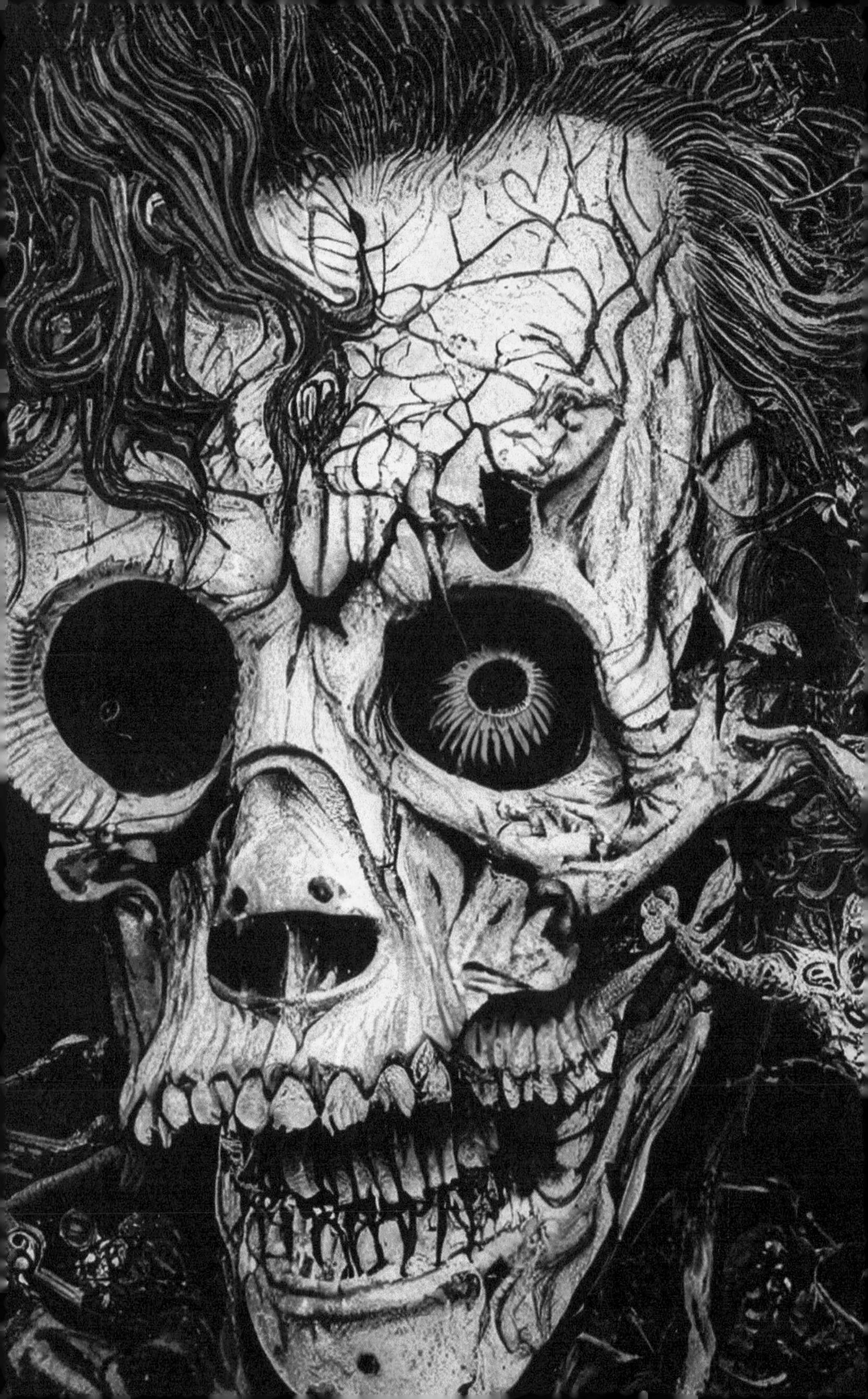

AUTHOR INTERVIEW

JOSH MALERMAN

Feature by Janelle Janson

J osh Malerman stole my black, bookish heart with *Bird Box*, and he's had it ever since. His books include *A House at the Bottom of a Lake*, *Black Mad Wheel*, *Goblin*, *Inspection*, *Pearl*, *Unbury Carol*, and his latest, *Daphne*. Josh has a way with words and always has a story to tell. I am incredibly grateful to him for agreeing to chat with me.

JANELLE JANSON: Let's begin. How did you get started writing? Who or what inspired you to start?

JOSH MALERMAN: In fifth grade, I tried to write a book. Didn't finish it. Then later, comic books. Then in high school, a string of short stories. All horror. In high school, notebooks full of embarrassing poems. I still have those in the closet in my office. Then when I was twenty-nine, I wrote my first published novel in twenty-eight days. It was pure electric light, that experience. The world went white for me. I saw the ending of the book. Saw I was right there. Knew it. Wrote it. Couldn't sit still. And then after that, the doors were blown open.

JJ: What's your writing process?

JM: Each book finds its own routine and then sticks to it. *Bird Box* was written between 8 a.m. and noon every day. But the most recent book, *Incidents Around the House*, was written at 8 p.m. till midnight. So, I don't know going in what the routine will be, but once it establishes itself, it sticks. For endings, I think more in terms of landmark moments; I gotta get from here to there. With *Bird Box*, I had the birth scene in mind the whole time. It's not how the book ends, but in a way, that's the ending of the book.

JJ: That's such a great scene. What inspired you to write *Bird Box*?

JM: At the time, *Bird Box* was just the next idea to write. I'd had an image of a mother and two kids, blindfolded, navigating a river, and for whatever reason felt that was enough to start writing the book. Obviously by page two I started to ask myself, what are they fleeing? That's when a memory came to me of a high school teacher telling us a man might go mad if he even tried to contemplate infinity. So, what if there was a knock at the door? And what if I answered it and infinity was standing on the porch? What if infinity was personified so that it was a living, breathing concept that drove us mad when we saw it? From there, the book wrote itself.

JJ: Congratulations on your recent release of your latest novel, *Daphne*. I devoured the book and I want everyone to read it, so let's try something. Give me your one-sentence elevator pitch for the book.

JM: A seven-foot, denim-clad, whiskey and smoke smellin' slasher eviscerates the lives of the Samhattan High School girls basketball team as one player, Kit Lamb, struggles mightily with anxiety and begins to see Daphne as a living panic attack that gets closer the more she thinks about her.

JJ: Where did the character of Daphne come from?

JM: I'd been looking for an angle on anxiety for years. Panic attack as monster. It's a helluva thing to deal with because (as it says in the book) nobody ever gets through an anxiety attack by telling themselves they survived the last one. That's the nature of anxiety, right? You believe it every time it comes. In fact, I'd go so far as to say that with each bout of anxiety, the sufferer believes that this time is the worst they've ever had it, this is the most scared they've ever been. That's wildly fascinating to me.

Daphne, the woman, came to me fully formed. Some rock and roll makeup on the face of a blue corpse. Seven feet tall (which would awe the basketball players, no doubt). The lumbering way she just comes for you, bare hands. Daphne's my living panic attack.

JJ: Do you believe in ghosts or monsters? Is Daphne a monster?

JM: I do. At the very least, I'm able to believe in them for the duration of a story, a film, a painting. I also have my own ghost story. A very scary one. Much fuller than anything corner-of-the-eye. We exchanged, we communicated. But maybe that's for another time. And Daphne is most definitely a monster. I just don't know if she's worse alive or dead.

JJ: I have to ask about your novel, *Ghoul n the Cape*. This is a story of epic proportions! Was this an important book for you to write?

JM: I'd had the idea for a while but I understood it was going to take some heavy lifting. It's the one book of mine I outlined. I just couldn't enter that story without some scaffolding. And yeah it's an important one for me. It's the ultimate optimist's horror novel. That doesn't mean it has a happy ending. That doesn't mean it's naïve. But it does mean the novel says you can come of age at any age.

JJ: What draws you to the horror genre?

JM: Anything goes in the genre. Literally anything. It's completely elastic and I feel like I can totally cut loose, and one book doesn't have to be anything like the other. Never. We never have to repeat ourselves in the genre. Horror is heaven for an imaginative person. Especially one who likes their imagination to play in the dark.

JJ: What is the first book that scared you?

JM: *The Face of Fear* by Dean Koontz. I didn't even know what I was getting into. I just knew it had a cool spine and so I asked Mom to get it at the bookstore. That's when I learned that there is no feeling like truly being scared. From then on, I hurried straight to the horror section of the bookstore, where all the spines were black with red letters.

JJ: What is your favorite book that you've written and why?

JM: *Wendy* for being the first. *Bird Box* for the fluidity of the rough draft. *Ghoul n' the Cape* for being the most "me." *Incidents Around the House* for scaring me.

JJ: What's the perfect novel?

JM: *Moby Dick*. Maybe.

JJ: Recommend a book you've read in 2022. Also, what book are you looking forward to?

JM: I read Grady Hendrix's *How to Sell a Haunted House* and while I wasn't surprised it was good, I was a little shocked at how emotional it made me. It's a fantastic rendering of a brother/sister dynamic and it'll have you thinking of your own family in new ways. And I can't wait to read Jonathan Janz's *Marla*.

JJ: What are you working on next? Any interesting announcements?

JM: *Spin a Black Yarn* is a collection of novellas slated to come out next year with Del Rey. That's all done and ready. Gonna edit *Incidents Around the House* soon. But I'm also eying a brand new one: *It Tolls For Thee*. I'm gonna write it any day now. I can feel it coming.

Daphne is on sale now, through Del Rey.*

*Purchase a signed copy of *Daphne* from VJ Books, the best place to buy signed books online, by scanning the QR code on the following page, or by going to vjbooks.com.

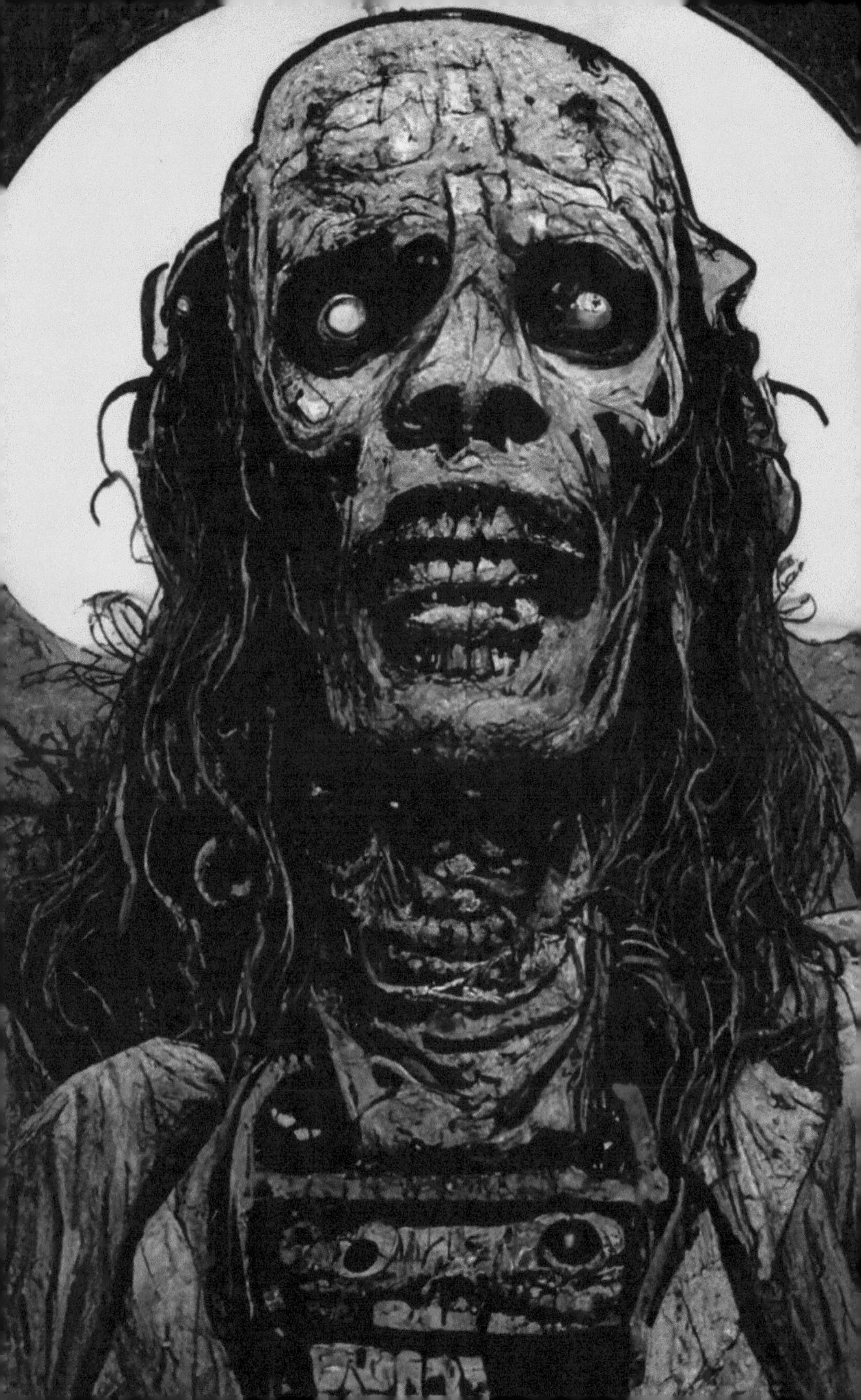

AUTHOR INTERVIEW

STEPHEN GRAHAM JONES

Feature by Jena Brown

Stephen Graham Jones loves horror, and his enthusiasm is contagious. He loves the creepy crawlies, the jump scares, and the things that go bump in the night, and his stories tap into our deepest fears. As he'll tell you, the world is a dangerous place and sometimes, the only way to cope with that danger is by confronting it.

To say he's prolific is an understatement. He's published dozens of novels and hundreds of short stories. His prose is razor-sharp prose and his narratives are tight, but it's his vivid characters that crawl under your skin and refuse to leave. I was delighted to sit down with Jones and talk about writing short fiction, his weirdest writing experience, and why he loves Halloween.

JENA BROWN: Thank you so much for making time to chat with us today! Can you introduce yourself to our readers?

STEPHEN GRAHAM JONES: Hey, I'm Stephen Graham Jones. I write horror novels. I read a lot of stories. I do comic books. I'm fifty years old and live in Boulder, Colorado. And I like trucks, boots, and slasher movies.

JB: You have a short story in Dark Matter's debut anthology, *Dark Matter Presents: Human Monsters,* coming from our new trade imprint, Dark Matter INK, this October. I don't want to give away too much, but can you give us a teaser by describing your story in five words?

SGJ: Me wanting to be Ketchum.

JB: Since we're starting with short fiction, do you have a favorite story length you like to write?

SGJ: Flash fiction is my favorite because from the moment you start, the story is ending. You get that pressure to find the resolution. But because the form is so compressed, you have to innovate to get more on the page. You have to write your story like a cornbread recipe. I love that standing invitation to innovate with form. It's probably my favorite thing about thing about storytelling, and flash fiction allows me to do that the most.

The first half of my career, I wrote so much flash fiction because my kids were young, and I'd always have Bounty Select-A-size paper towels around, and my stories could fit on one of those skinny pieces. Now that my kids can wipe their own faces, I don't have the paper towels around as much anymore, so I write a lot less flash fiction than I used to.

JB: Now that you have more time, do you tend to plot your books, or do you write by the seat of your pants? And does that change depending on what you're writing?

SGJ: It does change depending on what I'm writing. With short stories and flash fiction, and even somewhat with novels, I don't plan whatsoever. I just hear a voice and I follow it. I usually have a general idea of the situation, so I let that bloom and blossom and kind of go crazy. However, with the last 25%–30% of a novel, I have a mental to-do list of things that I have to tie up. I have to stop and figure out the sequence and how things feed into each other, generally by making a bullet list.

If I stumble into the end blindly, I'll get it on the page, but it won't be in the right order, or the events won't be set against each other in the right way, and I'll have to go back and undo it all so that I can put it back together in a better way. Of course, things never really work out exactly like they're written on my list, but it at least gives me some structure to work with.

Keeping those notes are also super helpful because as a writer, you want to always be moving forward. For example, if I'm writing a scene and someone uses a glass ashtray to brain someone, I usually haven't set the room up with props. But once that action takes place, I go back twenty pages and put the glass ashtray in the scene, or the candlestick over there. So I figure out what's going to happen and then go back to fill out the details. You do have to be careful because it's too easy to always be going back. You can fool yourself into believing you're making forward progress by being really rigorous and mulling the same thing over and over. You can be typing and working and thinking and writing, but not actually make progress get-

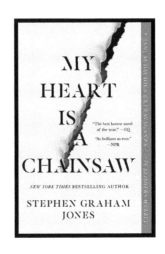

ting to the end. Which, that fear of the ending, in my case anyway, it's really fear of failure. The longer I can put off the end, the less risk it is for me.

JB: How do you deal with fear when it comes to writing? Do you ever struggle with things like writer's block or impostor syndrome?

SGJ: I just drink a lot of energy drinks and get going so fast that I can't think about that stuff. I've never actually subscribed to writer's block being a real thing. I think it's really just your standards being too high, and I think you can't make forward progress because you feel the whole world—critics and friends—are looking over your shoulder. And when you've got that many people watching you write, you can't type that next word because it's never going to be good enough.

I always find the trick for me is to lower my standards. I tell myself I'm just writing this for my cousin who is stoned twenty-four hours a day. And he's going to laugh at whatever I do. Then I can get some words down. They may not be good words, but I can fix them later. You can't fix zero words. I don't like to agonize over the words, but I do agonize over the order of words, the syntax, because the prose is where the story happens. But not to the point where I can't make forward progress.

As far as impostor syndrome, I don't know if I've ever had it. I mean, I always feel like a faker and not worthy. I think that's just part of being human. But to me, art is wrestling with beauty. And to wrestle with beauty, you have to inflate your ego up so that you're at the same stature as beauty. I think for artists to create, they have to fake like they're bigger and better than they are.

JB: Is there anything you're afraid of?

SGJ: Everything really. I think that's why I'm a horror writer. Because I walk through the world with constant fear. I'm afraid of the dark, of losing people close to me. When I take the trash out and it's close to dusk, my heart's beating because I think there's probably going to be a werewolf out there. If someone is late coming to my house, my first thought is: I bet they got picked up by a UFO on the way. To me, the world is nothing but dangers, so I try to deal with it by writing horror.

JB: Since this interview is going to appear in our Halloween issue, I have to ask: What's your favorite part of Halloween?

SGJ: The freedom to wear masks and not have people look askance at me. I love to drive around in a mask that I can safely see out of. There's not a lot of those. But I love to pull up next to somebody and watch as they just look over, and then look again. I just ordered another mask this morning. There wasn't much that was nice about the pandemic, but I liked that we got to cover half of our face because I never know what to do with my mouth. So, masks are my favorite.

I also love going to haunted houses. I love thinking about the possibility that it's all gone off the rails, because I know it's an attraction and there's insurance and safety measures. But what if there's really a crazy person loose in there? What if it's like that movie *Hell Fest*, and there's a real killer mixed in with all these actors? That's the scary stuff.

I also have one of those thirteen-foot skeletons, and a Nightcrawler

from Spirit Halloween; you know, the guy with a long mouth on all fours in a cloak. There's a light sensor in Nightcrawler, so when people get within like twelve feet, he jumps and roars. He's legitimately scary. That to me is what Halloween is all about. Fun. That's what I love.

JB: Before we go, let's have some fun. You and three slasher villains from pop culture are planning a Halloween party. Who are your accomplices? What are you planning? And who do you invite?

SGJ: The first person I team up with is Mandy Lane from *All the Boys Love Mandy Lane*, because she is really good at misdirection. I think she'd be a good plant. I'd also pick Stu from *Scream* because I think he'd be fun at a party, and he'd be stabby, which is fun at a Halloween party. I don't know if this counts as a slasher, but the clown from *Stitches* would be my third pick. I'd have him walking around, not talking to anybody, maybe serving cupcakes or carrying one of the guns from *Killer Clowns from Outer Space*, trapping people in cotton candy or something.

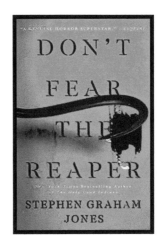

I would invite high schoolers. I'm not saying I want high schoolers to die. I just think high schoolers are kind of the ideal age group for a slasher victim pool, you know?

JB: I know you're limited on what you can say, but can you tease our reader's a bit about your upcoming book, *Don't Fear the Reaper*. What was it like being back with Jade in Proofrock?

SGJ: I'm going to miss her so much when I'm through with this trilogy because she's a real person to me. At the same time, she's a characters in a horror story, so I have to be brutal and cruel to her as well. But being back in that world and writing it was wonderful.

What I can say about *Don't Fear the Reaper* is that I really studied *The Empire Strikes Back* and *The Two Towers* a lot because I wanted to understand how the middle installment of trilogies work.

JB: What's next?

SGJ: My audiobook *The Babysitter Lives* just came out, and issue one of my new monthly comic book *Earth Divers* just released. *Don't Fear the Reaper* comes out in February 2023, and I have another novel in the queue that I can't talk about yet.

The Babysitter Lives (Simon & Schuster) and issue one of *Earth Divers* (IDW Publishing) are available now.

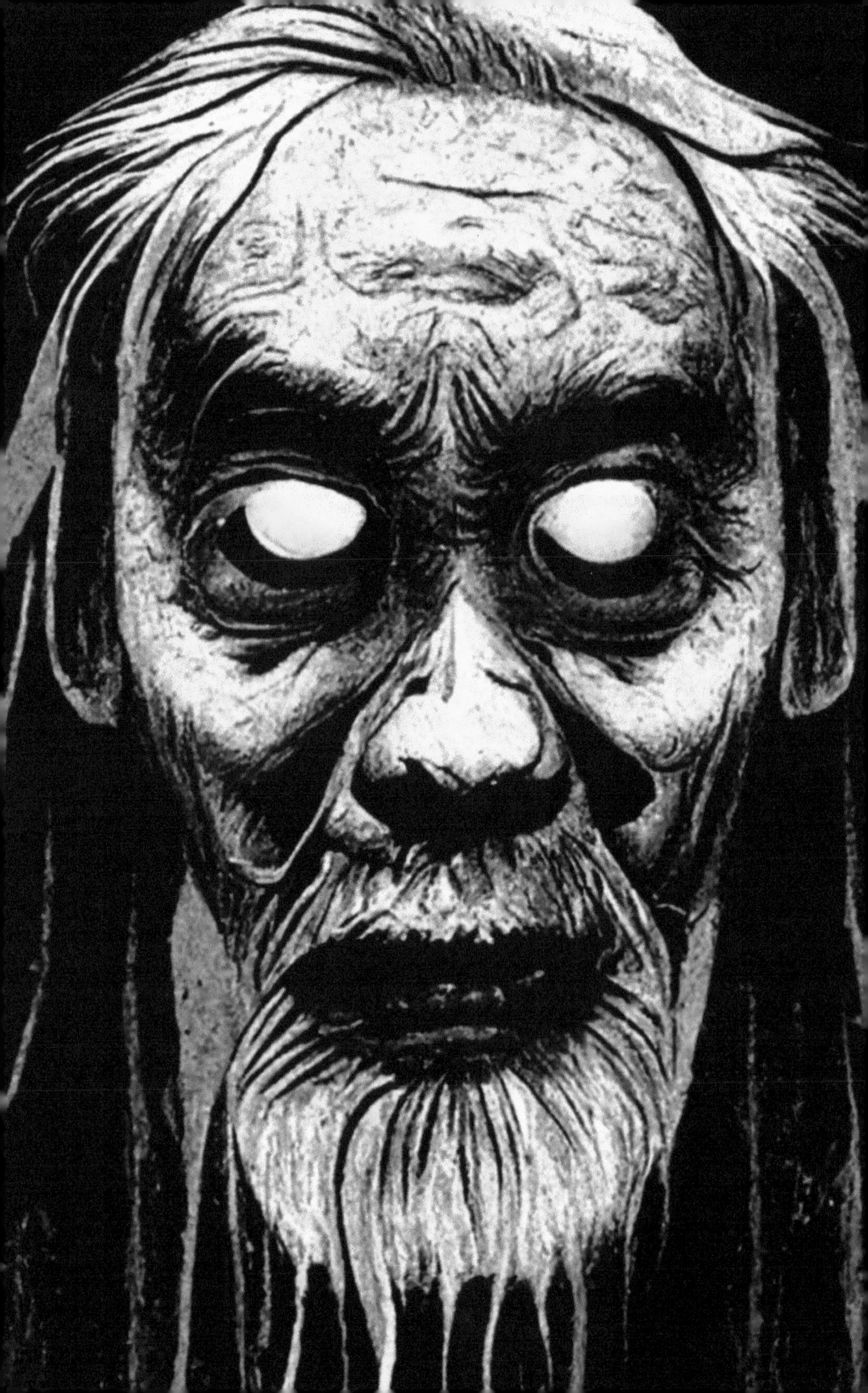

REPRINT STORY

Originally Published by The Dread Machine

WHAT WE LOOK FOR AT THE NIGHT MARKET

by Ai Jiang

When meeting death, there is first a moment of confusion—a space in-between where ghosts wander—wonder—until they do not. Guilt is a fickle thing—forgetting is even trickier.

There are four of us.

We split into pairs: two on one motorcycle, two on the other. We settle behind mysterious riders with scarred helmets that Ingri had waved down.

On foreign land, it is difficult to tell where one might arrive even when you offer a concrete destination or point on a map. "There. That is where I want to go." Often, where you want to go is never where you end up. Often, what you want to let go of never leaves you. Will the guilt ever leave me?

"Last group there has to treat us all!"

Jiken's voice rings like bell chimes, hanging in the air even as their rider kicks the engine into gear. Ingri's laughter fades with the echo of Jiken's words. The three shadows disappear in the rising fog mixed with the bike's roaring smoke, leaving the rest of us basking under the streetlamp light, which acts like an invisible dome, shielding us from the unknown. I want to reach out, hold onto the back of their bike, but they are already gone.

The last thing I see before they disappear into the fog is Ingri's tears, catching in the bike's exhaust fumes.

Lotia digs her nails into the thick fabric of the rider's jacket in front of me. They hardly make a dent. I wrap my hands around her waist. She's shaking even though I am the one sitting on the back edge, almost falling. I cannot help but imagine a sinister smile, a humanized Cheshire cat, on the rider's obscured face. Would it be scarred, too, like their helmet?

I hold on to Lotia tight, but it is as if she is not there. Her vanilla scent wafts around me, a comfort, though I do not feel her warmth. Always with a small, intimate smile on her face, like she is keeping a secret. But today, she does not turn in front of me. Is she still smiling?

"Hurry! We must arrive first," Lotia says.

What is the hurry when there is no time remaining?

My arms loosen, her presence only an echo—the rider, too, a shadow.

Why is there such loneliness in togetherness? Such ethereal melancholy with loss?

Such eerie idealism in sentimentality?

The rider swerves dramatically, veering at such sharp angles when rounding each street bend. I think I might just fall off, my friend's figure wedged between us like a rag doll. I avoid her flopping head. Her skull rattles in place, lifeless. Only imagination, I suppose.

"When will we get there?" I ask.

"We are already here," says the rider.

I swear there is a razor tooth smile glinting under the helmet, taking up the entire face, fractured by its scars. The longer I stare, the more clearly my face reflects on the black plastic surface, as if I am the rider, shuttling us all towards uncertainty.

As we move through the fog, Lotia's figure becomes translucent—the rider too. The only one still solid is me. I let go of the Lotia, leaning back, but I do not fall.

At the night market, we are all ageless.

I call for a bottle, and then another. I never drank before. But there is something about this place that makes nothing matter.

The vendor stares at me for a second, skeptical. But business is all the same. There does not seem to be such a thing as responsibility here. The bottle cap pops open, tumbling onto the rotting wood countertop before he swipes it from the surface.

"I will open the other one when you are finished with the first."

The words make him sound good-natured, but really, it seems the man questions my tolerance. If I can withstand his stench of rotten fruit, sickly sweet and sour, I can withstand two bottles. If I can withstand the ominousness of my friends' retreating figures disappearing in the fog, the burn of alcohol is nothing in comparison. If I can withstand my friends being only echoes… In the night market, it all feels like nothing anyhow.

I raise the bottle to my mouth in a slow, deliberate motion. I drink with my head turned to the side, my eyes drawn to the corner where the vendor stands, staring with arms across a deflated chest, almost concave like his cheeks. Looks like my father. Probably an alcoholic too.

"Now, the second," I say.

"Pay first."

A sigh escapes my lips. I belch. My father hated when I did that. Laughter bubbles up my throat. My elbow drops onto the decaying wood, a bill held out loose between my fingers. His fingers brush my knuckles as he grabs the money. I do not feel him. The vendor's eyes widen.

"You should not be here."

Flies huddle around the warmth of a light bulb. Their buzz bounces off the inside of my ears. The air is suddenly frigid. With goosebumps rising, my skin pulls taut against the bone.

The man's face ripples and continues to ripple until I can no longer tell whether he is fifty years old or five. Someone I missed—someone I am still missing. Father, father, father.

The crowd roaming the rest of the night market moves like a sea with disjointed waves. Jiken and Lotia's figure breaks through, beckoning me with their hands.

"Let us go to the river!" Their voices blend and merge until I can no longer tell which sound belongs to who.

My mouth drops open, but I have no voice. The river is dangerous. None of us can swim. A silent warning hangs lost in the air. My friends disappear into the crowd of shadows. They are residents here, but I am just a visitor. Jiken used to sling his arm around the rest of us whenever we hung out. Now he only holds Lotia's hand.

There is a certain loneliness—and invisibility—to the most crowded of places. There is nothing to the warmth of the collected bodies of strangers, not really.

"What would you like to buy?"

Tendrils of shadows writhing on skewers lie on the table next to cups and bowls of white powder. Raw blotched flesh sits out on ice, not for consumption, but to show how deep bruises penetrate, how deep we remember. Melting sweetness drips onto hard, tar ground, sizzling on contact; the sweetness always evaporates before the tar softens. Does it ever soften?

My father was like tar, my mother like melting sweetness... until she, too, became tar, and I the blotched flesh they never seemed to remember. Their bodies laid in odd angles in the bedroom, bottles broken, still clutched between dirty claws. I watched, hidden behind the door sitting ajar, then I fled. The image never leaves me.

The vendor smiles—no teeth—an elastic chasm. The flesh and sweetness they are selling is their own. The powder is made from their teeth, filed to nothing—lost from protecting oneself or lost to obedience? Tar always wins. You get stuck in the liquid, like my parents. The vendor looks like my mother.

"Why are you still here?"

I step back. There is nothing I want here. This is a place for remembering, but I wish only to forget.

Along the bridge by the water, two shadows run—sometimes separate, sometimes intersecting. Jiken and Lotia. Where is Ingri?

I run to join them, but by the time I reach the bridge, they are gone. My heart quickens as my eyes search around me. Shadows move in both directions on the bridge. None look like Jiken or Lotia. I look down. I can still see my hands.

Laughter drifts in the wind and guides my eyes towards the dark waters below me. Blood pounds in my ears. Something burns in my throat. The way it laps against the grass sounds like a somber song, like sloshing through mud, like stepping into and out of wet tar.

Three figures stand together by the water, daring one another to dive in, but knowing if they do, they will never resurface. Suddenly, I am with them, watching as one tips over the edge. Was it Jiken? By accident? On purpose? And then another, Lotia. To be a savior? Or to their end together? My arms remain glued to my sides as I watch the two thrash. Ingri reaches her hand towards them—too late.

With a shaking hand, I grab Ingri and pull her from the river, knowing if I do not, she too would disappear into the tar.

"Dia!" says Ingri. She tries to pull free. My fingers cut into her skin.

"You cannot. You cannot. You cannot." My voice echoes in my head.

Ingri looks back to the river. The water now still, but her tears disturb its surface. Together, we flee, diving back into the crowdedness of the night market where no one can hear us breathe.

We are in a place where the dead do not remain dead and the living cannot tell otherwise, nor can the dead, until someone breaks the spell—always by accident.

I return to the drink vendor, my father.

"How did you die?" asks my father, his figure a translucent shadow.

He clutches a broken bottle in his hand, re-enacting almost the same posture he died in. I shudder when he raises it. The fine hairs on my skin stand as he points the sharp edges towards me. I try to take a step back, but my feet remain planted as he moves closer.

The shadows of the night market move behind me. I feel the light, cold wind that brushes my back when they walk past. Jiken and Lotia are somewhere in these waves, no longer lost in the water. But Ingri and I cannot join them yet. "I did not."

My father laughs.

"Is it not great to be alive?" he says—the same words he said before he passed. Though in this context, the meaning seems so different. "Is it not great...to remember?"

I raise my hand and place it over his, a stark beige against his gray, and I force him to lower the bottle.

"No, but I will not forget."

And they all disappear—my father, the shadows, the stilling of rippling waves after the unexpected fall, the splash as Lotia dives in after Jiken with her small smile, Ingri's defeated expression, the silence when neither came back up.

We cannot help but return to the places that stay with us, for one reason or another. Ingri and I cannot help but return to the night market, looking to forget something we will never be able to forget, hold on to people we abandoned.

I sit by the water, my feet hovering by the edge, held above the singing wavelets. I see bubbles drifting upwards from the dark surface, but they never break through.

Behind me, the night market comes back alive. The vendor has a different face when Ingri approaches, but her heart is harboring the same guilt as mine. Who will she meet there other than Jiken and Lotia? Her parents? A lover? Another stranger she has kept from us?

My legs withdraw back onto land, toes curling, nails digging into the soil, gripping onto the edge. I reach my hand in the water, hoping to pull out something I cannot find among the crowd, vendors, and sold goods I leave behind. But I feel nothing but echoes. At least this time, I am not fleeing.

The color of my hand disappears when it enters the water, becoming half a shadow. Something takes hold, but I do not flinch or pull back. My body tilts forward. It does not fall but stays suspended in the air. I see Lotia's face staring back at mine, the same small, intimate smile on her lips. Jiken hovers behind her, laughter tinkling like bells, their fingers interlaced.

Soon, Ingri will take my spot, but I will no longer be here by then.

COMING 10.18.22

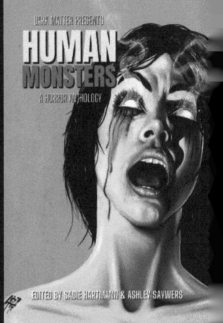

PRE-ORDER NOW

DARK MATTER PRESENTS: HUMAN MONSTERS is a new horror anthology from our trade imprint Dark Matter INK. The anthology features 35 brand new tales of terror from some of the best authors in the business. Get yours today at darkmattermagazine.shop

Dark Matter INK is a trade imprint of Dark Matter Magazine

AUTHOR AND ARTIST BIOS

For more information about the authors and artists featured in this issue, including bios, photographs, and web links to relevant work, please visit:

darkmattermagazine.com/authors
darkmattermagazine.com/artists

AUTHOR BIOS

ARTIST BIOS

SUBMIT TO DARK MATTER MAGAZINE

For more information on how to submit fiction or artwork to *Dark Matter Magazine*, please visit our submission guidelines page:

darkmattermagazine.com/submission-guidelines

BECOME A DARK MATTER MEMBER

Purchase a *Dark Matter Magazine* Membership for as low as $1.00 per month, and receive valuable perks like a digital subscription, free Audio Edition downloads, and up to 20% off all items in the store. To learn more, visit:

darkmattermagazine.shop/pages/memberships

FRIENDS?

 Get our emails

 Follow us on Twitter

 Like us on Facebook

 Follow us on Instagram

Get 20% Off New Books
Join the club
with a Dark Matter Membership.

Don't just subscribe. Save. Multiple plan options allow you to choose the membership that's right for you.

Plans start at $1.00 per month

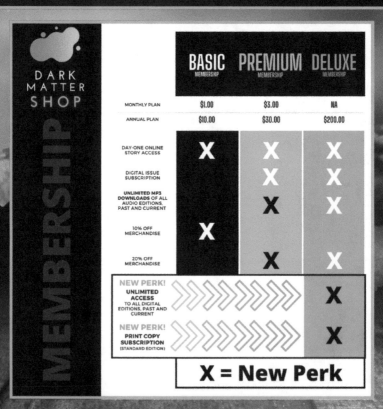

DARK MATTER SHOP

MEMBERSHIP

	BASIC MEMBERSHIP	PREMIUM MEMBERSHIP	DELUXE MEMBERSHIP
MONTHLY PLAN	$1.00	$3.00	NA
ANNUAL PLAN	$10.00	$30.00	$200.00
DAY-ONE ONLINE STORY ACCESS	X	X	X
DIGITAL ISSUE SUBSCRIPTION		X	X
UNLIMITED MP3 DOWNLOADS OF ALL AUDIO EDITIONS, PAST AND CURRENT		X	X
10% OFF MERCHANDISE	X		
20% OFF MERCHANDISE		X	X
NEW PERK! UNLIMITED ACCESS TO ALL DIGITAL EDITIONS, PAST AND CURRENT			X
NEW PERK! PRINT COPY SUBSCRIPTION (STANDARD EDITION)			X

X = New Perk

only at
darkmattermagazine.shop